Discreet in the Heat

A Bess Bullock Retirement Home Mystery

by

Allen B. Boyer

For information, email Cozy Cat Press, cozycatpress@aol.com or visit our website at: www.cozycatpress.com

COZY CAT
PRESS

ISBN: 978-1-946063-73-1
Printed in the United States of America

10 9 8 7 6 5 4 3 2 1

For Katherine Savery Gray—a creative muse gone too soon

Chapter 1: THE TWO WORD KNOCKOUT

When she worked as the only female police officer in her hometown of Venton, Bess Bullock knew a few male officers who liked to keep in shape by boxing. To the best of her recollection, there were more than a few who gauged how tough they were by the number of blows they could take to the head. Bess, who had always been small in stature, never considered stepping into the gym to partake in such macho gamesmanship. On occasion, she'd overhear some of her coworkers describing what it was like to take a strong punch to the head. How they could hear bells ringing in their ears. How it felt like there was a butterfly stuck in their head. A few even described a sensation that the world was spinning around them right before their eyes went shut. The reason for this flood of recollections about boxing was sitting directly in front of Bess.

Her only daughter, Samantha, had just finished conveying some surprising news. It was the kind of news that made Bess feel like a fighter who'd been clocked in the head once too often. Her ears rang and her head swirled and she was grateful to be sitting down. While she stared at her daughter, Bess began to rub her forehead with one hand in an attempt to ward off a headache.

She looked at Samantha, narrowed her eyes and asked her daughter to repeat her news again. She watched Samantha shift a little in her chair, clear her throat and look down at the floor the way she always did before delivering news she knew her mother wouldn't like. It was the same set of nervous mannerisms Bess saw twenty years earlier when Samantha was a nervous elementary school girl.

"I'm pregnant," Samantha said again and her eyes quickly fixed on her mother.

Bess's eyes instinctively turned to her daughter's ring finger and noted the absence of anything on it. Her thoughts then shifted to an obvious question.

"Who's the father?"

"A friend," Samantha replied and she folded her arms nervously like she always did when she knew Bess was unhappy. "That's all I can say, mother. I'm not going to give you a name or a detailed account of our relationship. He's just…a friend."

"And…" Bess began, but found her tongue and her thoughts muddled.

"And what?" Samantha asked.

"And…are you going to marry him?" Bess asked.

"He's not ready to make that kind of commitment," Samantha replied and she rubbed her arms as if she were catching a chill on this warm summer day.

"Well, apparently he was ready to commit *something*," Bess smirked.

"Mother!" Samantha scolded.

Bess reached out and gently placed her hand on her daughter's hand.

"The last time you were pregnant you were going through a divorce," Bess stated and she let out a long sigh. "I remember helping you raise one child when you didn't have a husband. It was hard on you…caring for a baby by yourself. I just don't want you to have to raise another child alone. Besides, at my age I'm afraid I won't be much help."

"I know," Samantha nodded. "I'm not going to marry someone I don't love, mother. I told him about the pregnancy and he's been very supportive of my decision to have this baby. I also told him I don't want any money. I'm a successful business woman and a mother to one daughter. I can make it on my own with a second child."

"So you *are* going to raise this child without a father…like Nicole?" Bess asked, referencing her favorite and only granddaughter.

"I know how much work it will be but I think I can do it," Samantha observed.

"Remember, you were younger when you had Nicole," Bess pointed out, referring to her only granddaughter. "We were both younger. It will be hard to do this again. Being a single parent to a baby is demanding."

"I won't be alone," Samantha said.

"You mean Nicole?" Bess asked.

"I think she'll be a good big sister," Samantha smiled. "I'll teach her to change some diapers. She can help me in lots of ways."

"I'm certain she will," Bess nodded. "Just don't ask too much of her. As for me, I was there for you when you needed my help with Nicole when she was a baby. I was there every time you called. I may be older but I'll still try to do what I can."

"I'm not asking for your help," Samantha stated, and she gently laced her fingers between her mother's fingers. "I'm asking you to be happy about my news. You're going to be a grandmother again. Aren't you happy about that?"

Bess forced her lips into a smile and kept it on for the rest of the visit. On some level, she felt like her daughter was making a mistake but chose not to say so. After a few minutes, Bess's husband, Chet, entered the room carrying two small suitcases. He placed them on the floor next to the front door, put both hands on his hips, and smiled at Bess.

"All packed for our big trip," he announced.

"Is today the day?" Samantha asked.

Bess could only nod to Samantha's question. Her mind quickly turned from a new grandchild to another change in her life. She glanced at the packed bags by the front door and mashed her lips together. She knew that the day had come for a change in her life. Her heart told her it was not going to be a pleasant change.

Chapter 2: LEAVING DOGWOOD LANE

At exactly noon, Bess and Chet stepped out of their ranch home on the grounds of the Honey Hills Retirement Community and walked down their driveway. Once at the edge of the street, they put their suitcases down and waited. Together they stood by the street, each with a small suitcase, squinting up at the warm morning sunshine. It was June, which meant that a hot summer sun was always ready to greet anyone who stepped outside.

After a few seconds their eyes glanced up and down their street at an odd sight. They smiled to their neighbors, who were also standing in front of their homes also with suitcases. To the average person, Bess thought, this would appear to be some kind of mass evacuation occurring on Dogwood Lane. Unfortunately, Bess knew better.

The longer they waited the warmer the air became. A church bell in the distance sounded that it was officially twelve o'clock. Bess, Chet and their neighbors remained outside, a few of them wiping sweat from their brow, folding their arms, and occasionally calling across the street to each other. No one went back into their house. No one stepped into the street. They all remained on their properties, in anticipation of something that was about to happen.

"Another hot day," Chet sighed, wiping his forehead. "They say this heat wave is setting records everywhere. It's been one terribly hot summer so far."

Bess did not reply to the statement. Her mind was occupied with what was about to happen. Her eyes grew teary. She turned and her gaze lingered on her front yard, her front porch and her house. The longer she stared the more she could feel her heart break.

"I don't want to leave," Bess sighed, feeling one tear roll down her cheek.

"It's only for a few weeks," Chet softly offered, his hand gently rubbing her back.

"I know," Bess sniffed, glancing over to him. "It's just…well…I already lost one home when I agreed to my daughter's wishes to move here. Even though it was a few years ago, I can still recall how painful it was for me to say goodbye to my first home. I guess some of those feelings are coming back to me this morning."

"Really, Bess," Chet smiled, his optimism on clear display. "We haven't been living in our little home for all that long."

"This is where we lived right after our wedding," Bess observed. "Now that we have to move to the Honey Hills Retirement Home's main building…well….it just won't feel the same to me. I know we lived in the main building before we were married but…I've just grown accustomed to spending our days going anywhere or doing anything we wish. I like living on a whim, Chet. I'm worried about all the rules and schedules we'll have to follow. I don't want our married life to lose its magic by going back to a place where nurses tell us what to do day and night."

"Remember…this is *only* temporary," Chet observed and he reached over and took her hand and gently squeezed it. "We'll be alright, dear. They say it'll be like a new house when we come back. They'll paint some walls, check the pipes and fix what they need to fix. Maybe they'll even give us a new rug. It'll be a brand new place for us to move back to. It'll be our chance for a new beginning, too."

"But I don't want a *new* beginning," Bess quickly answered. She looked at Chet. "I don't want a *new* house, either. I like our home and I like our life the way it is. Just because something's old...doesn't mean it needs to be changed to make it better."

"You have to try something new before passing judgment on it," Chet sighed and he wrapped his arm around Bess's waist before giving her a hug.

"I know you're right," Bess said, glancing back up the driveway at their house again. "It's just that...I'm going to miss our home. I've already made a promise to my gardens that I'll check on them every morning. My body may be moving into the main building but my heart...my heart will stay here on Dogwood Lane."

No sooner did those words leave her lips than a small bus appeared at the corner of their street, turned and slowly drove up. The vehicle stopped right in the middle of Dogwood Lane and the driver gestured for Bess, Chet and all their neighbors to board.

"Good morning, folks," a chubby chipper man said from behind the wheel. His face was bright red. His hair was white and lay like a cumulus cloud on his head. A pair of sunglasses concealed his eyes, but his smile and good nature were clearly visible to all who were boarding the bus. Most of the residents from Dogwood Lane replied with a polite smile but not much else. Once everyone was seated, Bess didn't hear anyone speak.

"Ahh...the air conditioning feels good," Chet sighed, dropping into the seat next to Bess. "I don't know about you but I was starting to melt out there."

Bess remained silent. She kept her eyes focused on their small ranch home. Soon the bus's engine roared and she felt it move. She watched her house grow smaller as the bus began to pull away from Dogwood Lane. When it turned the corner, she spotted her two gardens in the backyard. She had a lump in her throat and she felt like a mother being separated from her children. She turned in her seat and promised herself that she would return to water and weed her gardens no matter how hot the temperature.

"I'll be back," Bess whispered to herself.

The bus turned onto Magnolia Lane and accelerated down the street that led to the main building of the Honey Hills Retirement Center.

"I don't know why they're doing this," she heard one woman grumble from the back row of the bus.

"I heard a rumor that radon levels were high in our homes," another woman across from Bess observed. "That's something that needs to be addressed, if true."

"We all do have French drains in our basements," a man from across the aisle nodded.

"I heard it was the plumbing that needed some attention," another neighbor spoke up. "I was a plumber and I've always said they need to replace those old metal pipes with PVC pipes. After all, plastic does last longer, you know."

The engine hummed louder when it pulled out from a stop sign, discouraging anymore conversations. Like it or not, Bess had come to grips with the fact that she and Chet were simply going to downsize for a few weeks. Her quiet days of working in her garden, reading books on her porch, taking leisure evening walks and chatting with neighbors were gone. Instead of indulging in such pleasant diversions, she would be surrounded by a wide range of new residents, the smell of bland meals and a few well-meaning nurses who tended to foster a feeling of helplessness rather than independence. The only positive thing about the situation, Bess concluded, was that she would also be surrounded by new faces, which always held her interest.

Observing people and learning their stories was a hobby that Bess enjoyed. As a former police officer, she always had a good eye for studying people and learning things about them. She found that a person's eyes, movements, words and expressions always led her to discover curious things. Her ability to read people and make deductions about them was a gift she had nurtured for a lifetime. With her eye for studying the behavior of others, she knew moving to the main building of the Honey Hills Center would be anything but boring. *After all*, she thought, *behind every curious behavior was a hint of a mystery waiting to be resolved.*

Without warning the bus slowed and turned into the parking lot. The building loomed just ahead of them. What looked different was a new addition to the main building. A ten-story tower that poked out of the main building and stretched up to the sky. The windows flickered in the morning sun like diamonds. As they drew closer, Bess was impressed by the size of the structure.

"I wonder how many residents live up there?" she asked to no one in particular.

"They just built it," a voice replied. "Maybe no one lives there, yet."

Suddenly the bus stopped at the entrance to the main building. As they filed out the door of the bus, Chet and Bess grabbed their suitcases and stood in front of the double doors.

"Are you ready for this?" Chet asked.

Bess smiled back and nodded.

Together they carried their suitcases off the bus, through the main entrance and into a new adventure.

Chapter 3: TIME WITH FRIENDS

Whether she lived on Dogwood Lane, or in the main building of the Honey Hills Center, Bess knew she had one constant in her life. She knew she would still have a weekly meeting of Bridge Club to attend. She started going to Bridge Club meetings when she first moved into the retirement community. After a few meetings, Bess and the other three members of the club established a strong friendship. While they all enjoyed playing cards, their real pleasure came from the stories they told, the laughter they shared and the escape they provided from the daily routine.

On this particular morning, when the Bridge Club meeting got underway, Bess knew it would be hard to forget about her concerns. Her mind was still swirling with thoughts of moving away from her home, the new room they were being given, and her daughter's unexpected news about her pregnancy. While the other three members of the club, Flo Morgenstern, Alma Crisp and Ruth Gruber, simply sat and exchanged smiles and funny stories, Bess was not as willing to join in. Eventually they all grew silent and stared at her. She grinned back at them while a perfectly fine deck of cards sat at the center of the table waiting for the next round to be dealt.

"Is someone going to shuffle the cards or are we going to sit here and stare at each other?" Bess finally asked.

"You're a bit quiet this morning," Rose finally observed.

"I'm fine," Bess fibbed, forcing a smile across her cheeks.

"I think I speak for everyone here when I say welcome back to the main building," Alma grinned while picking up the cards and shuffling.

"Yes," Ruth added. "It's nice having you back with us, Bess."

"Even if it's only for a short while," Alma added.

"Thank you," Bess said, looking at each of her friends. "As you know, it was quite a surprise when they told us, but Chet and I are managing. We've had a few days to settle in."

"So the houses on Dogwood Lane are finally going to get some upgrades," Alma stated, before dealing the cards.

"It'll be like…getting a new home," Ruth grinned at Bess.

"That's what my husband keeps telling me," Bess quietly stated.

"I heard they needed upgrading," Alma nodded. "From what I've been told those homes have been there for a long time. They were due for some changes."

Bess quietly nodded, trying not to focus too much on the word "change."

"So how did this all come about?" Rose asked.

"Last month, Chet and I received a letter informing us that our house was scheduled to receive some upgrades," Bess reported. "From the carpeting to the countertops to the light fixtures, everything was going to be replaced. Even the walls will get a fresh coat of paint. I don't know what color but I do hope they ask me before they start painting. Blue is my favorite color."

"Did they say how long all this work would take?" Ruth asked.

"Less than a month is what we were promised," Bess replied, glancing down at the cards she was dealt. "I still don't know why they're changing things. Chet and I were perfectly happy with our house. I guess they need to keep things looking sharp for the next generation of retirees. You know, ladies, there's an illusion that is created when you spend your days outside of this main building. Living on Dogwood Lane, sometimes you forget you're part of a retirement community. You simply don't see the main building so it's easy to forget. When something like this happens…it takes away that illusion."

"So where are you and Chet going to live while this work is being done?" Alma asked before playing her first card.

"They moved us into a very nice apartment in a place called the Tranquil Tower," Bess replied.

All three ladies' mouths dropped open when Bess finished her statement.

"You mean those new luxury apartments?" Ruth asked, her eyebrows going up.

"Yes," Bess nodded.

"Wow!" Alma laughed. "Aren't you living in style, Bess? They just finished construction on those apartments about a month ago. I heard those rooms have big screen TVs, new carpeting, new beds, and the best views around. Even the recliners have a massage function, or so I was told. I spoke to a couple I know who just love living in them. They tell me that the Honey Hills hopes those rooms will attract more wealthy couples to live here."

"We're on the top floor and the room is very nice," Bess said. "I mean, in addition to the TV and the massaging chairs, the space is lovely. The first time I stepped into the living room and walked over to this huge bay window, well…the view took my breath away. We have a wonderful vantage point of the grounds from our room. If I look hard enough, I can even see my house and my gardens from that window. Despite so many nice features in the apartment, I must admit that my heart still aches for my home. So it looks like Chet and I are…stuck here."

"Stuck? In that plush apartment?" Flo giggled.

"Don't think of it as being stuck," Rose suggested.

"Yes," Alma nodded, pointing across the table to Bess. "Think of it as…a vacation."

"I'm trying to do just that," Bess smiled, and her eyes scanned the faces of her friends and stopped on the one person who was noticeably silent. "You haven't had much to say, Flo. Do you have any advice to sustain me while I'm living here?"

"Yes," Flo mumbled. "Play cards and quit whining. You aren't losing a pet or a spouse. It's just a house, Bess. You'll move back."

"Really?" Bess asked, sitting up a little straighter. "Just a house? Is that how you see it? I know there will be memories I'll lose with the changes to my home. Every home holds special memories. How about your home, Flo? Don't you think there's something special about where you lived with your husband?"

"My husband always said a house is just a place to hang your hat," Flo sighed.

"I think a house is more than that," Rose stated. "I agree with Bess. A house is a place filled with memories. As you ladies know, I grew up on a farm in a beautiful home. I can still close my eyes and remember all the windows that faced the fields where our cattle and horses grazed. I can even smell my mother's pies baking in the kitchen. A home is more than walls and floors to me. It's a place that frames our memories, too."

"My dad was on the road a lot for work," Flo recalled. "Where I grew up it was just me and my mother around the house. When I think about it, we never lived in one place long enough to make any memories."

"I grew up in an apartment most of my life with my mother," Alma shrugged. "It was small, but I still smile when I think about it. My mother and I laughed a lot in that little place."

"I also have good memories of the home where my husband and I raised our family," Bess explained and she paused for a minute to collect her thoughts. She glanced down at the wedding ring on her finger and flickers of happy memories filled her head.

"What are you thinking about?" Alma pressed.

"I was just thinking about how my home was like a companion to me," Bess explained, looking at her friends. "When we bought our house it was new and my husband and I were young newlyweds. As the years went by, both my home, my husband, and I started to show signs of aging. When my husband died and my daughter went off to college, that home became my protector of sorts. It shielded me from the worst storms and the coldest winters. I never had one thing break or go wrong with that house after my husband died. Maybe I've thought too long about it but...in many ways my home was like a faithful protector. Did anyone else feel that way?"

No one spoke in reply to her query. With her sentiments lingering in the air, not another word was uttered on the topic. A moment later all four ladies picked up the cards they were dealt and the first round of bridge began.

Chapter 4: AT HOME IN THE TRANQUIL TOWER

As the Bridge Club meeting evolved, it progressed from a philosophical discussion about homes to a rousing few hours of laugher and smiles while playing cards. When it was over, Bess offered to clean up while her friends left. Once the chairs were pushed in and the cards put away, she checked her watch. The time indicated she'd have to hustle back to the Tranquil Tower to pick up Chet.

Walking at a brisk pace, the advice from Alma rang in her mind.

"Arrive early for meals," Alma warned Bess. "Meals in the Dining Hall are served promptly. Don't be late or you won't get a good seat."

When she opened the front door to her apartment, Bess's eyes instinctively squinted at the bright sunlight. The large windows in the apartment faced east, causing the morning sun to illuminate the white walls and floor of their apartment. She spotted Chet stretched out on a brown leather sofa reading a book and wearing sunglasses.

"I love how the light fills this room in the mornings," Chet grinned, looking up from his book. "Starting off the day this way is gonna turn me into a morning person, Bess. If we were back in our old house, I'd have to go out on the back porch to get this much daylight to read by. I don't even need to wear my reading glasses in here. I can't believe I'm going to say it but…waking up to the sun is actually fun."

"This from someone who can sleep until noon," Bess grinned, her eyes scanning the room. "It is a lovely place they've given us. Although I heard that these rooms were built for attracting wealthy people to move in...not people like us."

"I think I have more than enough money from investments to live here," Chet quickly stated in what Bess thought to be an attempt to sway her sentiments.

"We have a home," Bess smiled and she pointed at her husband. "You don't need to brag about your money."

When she married Chet, after she moved to the Honey Hill Center, Bess never asked about his finances. In fact, she just didn't care. He was a sweet man, a contract lawyer by trade, and a good dancer. That's all she knew about him. They were both widows and lucky enough to fall in love again. What mattered most to her was in his heart, not in his bank account.

With the advice of Alma still fresh in her mind she quickly stepped into the bedroom to change from her comfortable blouse to something nicer. The bedroom, which was smaller than the one she was accustomed to in her old house, still smelled new. That "new" smell was an aroma she never tired of. She plopped her small suitcase on the bed, cracked it open and pulled out a white blouse to change into. Just as she slipped it on Chet wandered into the bedroom.

"Looks like another hot one out there," he observed, while glancing at himself in the mirror before running a comb through his thick white hair.

"It's hot every day," Bess nodded, stepping over to share the mirror with Chet. "I don't ever remember a summer being like this one. Every day is a scorcher. It wasn't this hot when I was a child."

"You know what I remember?" Chet recalled, "When I was a young man I had a friend named Arnie.

He lived on a farm. Every summer, on a day like this, me and some other fellas would walk across town to Arnie's farm. Once there we'd swim in a pond next to the barn. We'd swim until the sun went down. Good memories."

"I lived in the city," Bess sighed. "We didn't have a pool or a pond near our neighborhood. Sometimes, on hot summer days, a fire hydrant would be cranked open by a fireman. We'd have an hour to run through the cool water, but that didn't happen often."

Chet nodded then turned and looked at the bed. He started to laugh and pointed at her small suitcase on top of the bed. He turned to her and the expression on his face held a perfect blend of amusement and confusion.

"Why haven't you unpacked?" he asked.

"I'm not unpacking," she replied, tapping the top of her suitcase with one hand. "This place...this situation...it's only temporary. I'm treating our stay here like a vacation. I'm living out of my suitcase for a few weeks...and then we get to go back home."

"Suit yourself," Chet shrugged, dangling his finger to one side of the room. "More space in the closet for me."

Bess smiled at the comment and checked her watch.

"We'd better hurry up, Chet. We need to get to the Dining Hall," she advised. "Someone in my Bridge Club told me not to be late or there wouldn't be any good tables left for us to sit and I don't want to be stuck by the kitchen. I don't like seeing how they prepare my meal."

"Lunch? Already?" Chet frowned, checking his watch. "It's a bit early to eat. Besides, you know I like watching the business news at this time of the day."

"I'm afraid now that we're in the main building we're going to have a new schedule to keep," Bess sighed before closing her suitcase and placing it back on the floor next to the closet. "It appears that accountability comes with this fancy apartment. We get the good with the bad I'm afraid. Now we'd better get down there before all the tables are filled."

Chet shook his head and reluctantly followed her out the front door.

"You know what I'm hungry for?" Chet grinned as they walked down the hall to the elevator. "One of your delicious grilled cheese sandwiches. I'm already missing your grilled cheese with the extra cheese in it. You always make it not too burned. The bread is always just right. That's what I'm hungry for."

"Me too," Bess sighed. "Grilled cheese and some soup sounds just right to me. I hope they don't give us a heavy lunch. I'm still full from breakfast. Besides, I don't want to eat potatoes and meat this early in the day."

"I knew we weren't going to like this new schedule," Chet grumbled as they stopped in front of the elevator.

"I already miss being able to eat what I want…*when* I want," Bess observed, glancing at her watch again. "I can tell we'll need to be more conscious of the time while we stay here. I'm already looking at my watch more than usual."

"Yes, Bess, our easy-going days are done for now," Chet nodded while pressing the elevator button.

It was a concerning thought that Bess tried not to entertain as she waited for the elevator to arrive.

"Here less than a week," Bess grumbled, "and we're already rushing around."

"We'll adjust," Chet sighed.

"I already feel like our time is not our own," she complained. "I can tell I'm going to miss my carefree mornings, Chet. You know those mornings? The ones when I can read, or do gardening or stroll around the grounds for as long as I want. Now, all of our activities for the day will revolve around running to the Dining Hall for meals. Being held to this timetable is going to be like…having a job again!"

"How so?" Chet asked.

"Always being responsible for making appointments," Bess replied. "Even if those appointments are for dinner."

The elevator doors finally opened. As they stepped inside Bess continued to reflect on the leisurely rhythm to their lives on Dogwood Lane. A rhythm that she was certain they would miss.

A few minutes later, Bess and Chet arrived for lunch. The moment they stepped into the Dining Hall their view was filled by a large group of white heads seated at different-sized tables. Bess and Chet stood at the entrance, scanning the room for any sign of a vacant table for two. While they studied the room, Bess couldn't help but notice the details.

The decor of the Dining Hall was quite different from the days when she first moved to the Honey Hills main building. What used to be dark blue tones on the walls of the Dining Hall were now painted over with a bright white paint. A sky-blue rug replaced the dull crimson one. Even the uniforms of the servers were new. Like the homes on Dogwood Lane, change had also found its way to this part of the Honey Hills community.

"I see a table," Chet said, grabbing Bess by the hand.

Together they quickly converged on a small table for two in the back corner of the room. The table was fixed next to a bright red door with the word "EMERGENCY" printed in big white letters. Bess sat down while Chet, standing with his hands on his hips, stared at the door and began to laugh.

"Well, this is romantic," he grinned. "Just the two of us sitting next to the Emergency Exit. If there's a fire I'm sure we'll get trampled."

"I guess this is why my friend Alma said to come early," Bess said gesturing for Chet to sit down. She scanned the room one more time. "It looks like this is the only table left. Next time we'll have to come earlier."

The moment Chet sank into his seat a server arrived at their table. The server looked to be in her fifties, with a measured smile and salty black hair tightly braided on top of her head. She greeted them with a dour expression and placed a basket of dinner rolls at the center of the table before leaving.

"Well, at least we have warm rolls and a good view of the room," Chet pointed out, quickly reaching for the basket.

Bess smiled and turned to face the Dining Hall from her seat. From their secluded location, she noticed how they had a clear view of every face in the room. She looked across the table at Chet, who was busy chewing on his roll.

"I like this spot," Bess smiled.

Chet nodded and watched his wife look at the other tables. She leaned forward and rested her chin on the palm of her hand while studying the room and the residents.

"No wonder I didn't hear any complaints about this table," Chet observed.

"What do you mean?" she asked without looking at her husband.

"I know you too well, Bess," Chet laughed and he pointed around the room. "I know how you like to watch people. I can see the way you're looking around at them. So...while we're sitting here waiting for the food to arrive...can you entertain me?"

"How?" Bess asked.

"With a few of your clever insights," Chet said, finishing a dinner roll in two bites.

Bess felt her head tilt slightly to the side as she often did when she was confused by one of her husband's statements.

"Take a good look around the room," Chet instructed and he leaned forward with his elbows on the table. "Tell me if you see any *interesting* people in the room? A good story or two would help pass the time while we wait for our food."

She quietly unfolded her napkin and placed it on her lap before looking at him.

"Well…of course, every person looks interesting to me, Chet," Bess smiled.

"Look around," he said, egging her on with a wicked grin. "Who are the interesting people sitting near us for lunch? What details do you see with those curious eyes of yours?"

Bess cleared her throat, sat up a little straighter and adjusted her glasses.

"Well, let me see," she softly spoke.

Her eyes narrowed and she turned to her right where a group of unsuspecting residents were seated at a nearby table. Chet watched his wife focus on their faces. Her gaze lingered on them for a good minute, absorbing every feature and gesture. Bess reached for her water glass, took a sip, then smiled to her husband and gave him one quick nod.

"Well?" Chet asked, sounding eager for a report.

"Look at that table," she instructed. "Do you see that one man? The one with the bald head and the dark glasses? Do you see him?"

"Of course," Chet softly replied, turning in his seat. "He's wearing brown pants and is seated next to that woman in the maroon sweater?"

"That's the one," Bess nodded. "I watched him walk over to his table when we first arrived in the Dining Hall. I noticed how he moved with a slight limp. Did you notice that?"

Chet rubbed the whiskers on his chin for a few seconds.

"No," he shrugged, "I didn't notice him. I guess I was more focused on getting to this table before anyone else."

"When I watched him I thought his limp looked painful," Bess sighed and she shook her head after she revealed this detail.

"I didn't see him limp," Chet replied. "Besides, there are plenty of residents in a retirement home who have a limp. What can you learn from a person just because they have a distinct gait?"

"I don't know about other people...but here's what I learned," Bess began. "When we walked by his table I spotted a tattoo on his right forearm. It's very distinctive. Not too many residents have a tattoo like that one."

"So what makes it special?" Chet asked, adjusting his glasses to get a better look.

"It's the symbol for the United States Marines," Bess explained. "My father was in the Marines when he was a young man. You see my father had a medal that looked just like that man's tattoo. He kept it on the dresser in his bedroom. That's how I remember that symbol."

"Interesting," Chet nodded while taking a bite from another dinner roll.

"That's not all," Bess said and she leaned across the table before speaking. "I'll tell you what I think is *really* interesting. Do you see the shoes he's wearing? They look like corrective shoes to me. Can you see them?"

"Yes," Chet said, trying not to stare at Bess's subject.

"They look like the kind of shoes my father used to have," she continued. "My dad used to get shoes like that from the Veteran's Hospital in our hometown of Venton. If I remember correctly, he couldn't buy them in stores. He could only get them from the Veterans Hospital. Now with all those details in my mind, I'd wager a guess that the man we've been looking at may have been wounded while serving in the Marines, which is why he has that terrible limp and those special shoes."

"I see," Chet nodded. "So you think he's a wounded veteran?"

"I do," Bess nodded. "Now look at his wrist. If you look closely you'll see he's wearing a diabetes bracelet on his right wrist, just below the tattoo on his forearm. He probably has to be careful about what he eats when he comes here for meals."

"All that from a few seconds of watching a stranger," Chet grinned. "Not bad for a grandma! You never cease to amaze me with your ability to do that. It's like…magic!"

"I can assure you it's not magic," Bess quickly corrected while sitting back in her seat and placing a napkin on her lap. "It's just a snapshot of some details, Chet. When I see someone my mind races to fill in the blanks. Besides, I think my brain works faster when I'm hungry. Did you save me a dinner roll, dear, or did you eat them all?"

"There's one left," Chet said, handing her a basket containing the final roll.

"Thank you," she smiled, while buttering the roll. "Of course, I'd have to learn more details about that man to be sure…but it's a logical guess. From my experiences, my guesses tend to be correct."

Chet nodded, placed a napkin on his lap and sighed.

"When we eat lunch at home," Chet observed, "we'd always sit in front of the TV and watch the news. I know we both enjoy it. But after what you just did, I think this arrangement will make lunch lot more fun. Let's make a toast to more…entertaining lunches!"

Chet smiled before picking up his glass and reaching across the table with it.

"You make me blush, Chet." Bess grinned, casually picking up her water glass and gently tapping it against his. "While I'm happy to entertain you, lunch is not exactly the best venue for doing this. When I come here I'd like to be focused on eating rather than the people around us."

She took a sip of water and thought back to her younger days.

"You know, Chet," she began, "When I think back to my days as a police officer, I remember how some people I worked with thought being good at law enforcement was measured by how hard they could punch or how well they could shoot. I always thought I was good at my job because I had a keen eye for watching people closely and judging their character. There's a lot one can gleam from a person before making a sound judgment about them. You simply have to pay attention to them."

"You make it sound so easy," Chet laughed and he pointed around the room. "Is there anyone else in here that caught your eye?"

The very second he asked that question Bess noticed their server walking by to deliver another basket of dinner rolls to a table. It was the same middle aged woman who delivered rolls to their table when they first arrived. As before, she delivered them without a smile before waiting on another table.

"I noticed something about that woman when we first arrived," Bess said.

"Her?" Chet replied, pointing in the direction of the server. "She didn't say a word to us when we sat down. All she did was bring us dinner rolls. From what I recall, she didn't seem very pleasant, either. I smiled and she didn't even notice. What could you have possibly discovered about her...other than she has no personality and isn't very friendly?"

"You know what I learned?" Bess asked, her eyes watching the woman carry more baskets of rolls to other tables. Bess leaned in close to Chet. "I think that woman is a widow. I think she's a widow and I think it happened recently."

"And what makes you say that?" Chet asked.

"Just look at her," Bess nodded with a soft voice. "She has a diamond ring on her right hand. I also saw that she had a tan line on the ring finger of her left hand."

"How on earth did you notice that?" Chet grinned.

"I saw it when she put the basket of rolls on our table," Bess explained. "I suspect that the tan line is from wearing her wedding band on her left hand over the summer. Since she's here serving meals at lunch time, and not eating at home with her family, I'd be willing to guess she has no one to share meals with. Perhaps that's also why she hasn't really smiled at anyone while she passes out those baskets. Given her sullen demeanor, I believe she is grieving."

"Or her husband ran off with someone else," Chet added.

"Also a possibility," Bess said before pointing across the table to her husband. "The friends I know who got divorced, they tended to be more outgoing...determined to start a new life or try hard to take their minds off their problems. She just looks sad."

"Again...I'm impressed with what you find," Chet said, shaking his head and looking at his wife. "We've been married for a few years...but I never tire of your insights. Didn't you tell me once that you learned how to do this when you were a child?"

"That's right," Bess replied. "When I was a little girl I'd sit on the front porch with my daddy and I'd listen to him make all kinds of observations about people that walked by. When I got older he started teaching me to do the same thing."

"So you've always been able to find...how do you say it...the little details in people?" Chet asked.

"Pretty much," Bess said before taking a bite of her roll. "My father taught my older brother, Donald, and me to look at people and learn things about them from what we saw. Dad trained us how to do this at a very early age. What I can do now...I'm quite certain it's a combination of practice and good genes."

"Taking into account all that practice, and all those good genes, let me ask you one final question," Chet grinned, pointing at the choices on the menu. "Which meal do you think would be better to have...the chicken or the turkey? What details can you gleam before answering *that* question?"

"Oh, Chet," Bess laughed. "I'm not a food critic. I'm better at making judgments about people...not cooked birds."

She grew silent when the server returned, still wearing a dour expression on her face. Bess watched her turn to Chet and take his order. It was clear to her that the waitress was lost in her own thoughts. When it was her turn, Bess selected the chicken after hearing Chet order the turkey dinner. As with many things in life, it was the perfect way for Chet and Bess to play it safe and insure that they would have at least one satisfactory meal.

Thirty minutes later, after finishing their sizeable lunches, Bess and Chet decided to skip out on apple pie for dessert. As they left the Dining Hall, they lingered and exchanged a few pleasantries with some familiar faces at other tables. Eventually they made their way into the hallway where Bess spotted two familiar faces from Dogwood Lane. It was Anita and Cliff Mackley.

The Mackleys lived directly across the street from Bess and Chet. Anita was a pleasant person, always ready to share a bright smile and warm laugh. When speaking, Anita had the habit of squinting, which made it difficult to appreciate her blue eyes. Cliff, her husband, was shorter than Anita. He liked to chat and had a nervous habit of adjusting his glasses whenever he spoke.

When Anita and Cliff locked eyes with Bess, the expression on the Mackleys' faces told Bess that they were also having trouble adjusting to their new surroundings. As Bess and Chet approached, the Mackleys' faces melted into smiles.

"Hello, Mackleys," Bess said, with a wave.

"Hello, Bess," Anita replied, leading her husband up to where Bess and Chet were standing. "So how did you like that lunch?"

"I thought it was very filling," Bess sighed and she rubbed her slender stomach. "It was a little more than Chet and I are accustomed to eating."

"Grilled cheese is all I wanted," Chet grumbled.

"I agree," Cliff said, waving his finger at Chet. "I like a big breakfast and just a little something for lunch. They serve us way too much to eat around here, in my opinion."

"You're right about that, Cliff," Bess said. "A few more lunches like that one and I won't be able to fit in my clothes anymore."

"Perhaps the Honey Hills will buy you some new clothes, Bess," Anita laughed.

"I thought the turkey was good," Bess grinned. "Although Chet found the chicken a little tough for his liking."

"It needed more gravy," Chet complained. "Next time, I'll ask for some."

"This whole move has been a big adjustment for us," Anita observed.

"Accountability has been *our* biggest adjustment," Bess explained, taking Chet's hand. "The first morning I told him that we had to leave right away for breakfast, Chet was dumbfounded. We like to eat when we're hungry...not because the clock on the wall is telling us to run down to the Dining Hall."

"Yes," Chet nodded. "We just want our own timetable back."

"To be honest," Bess softly stated. "I miss my house already and it hasn't been all that long since we left."

"We miss our house, too," Anita nodded, taking one step closer. "Cliff and I like to watch the game shows on TV when we eat lunch. Now we're eating earlier, sitting with people we don't know...and there's no TV to watch!"

"Adjustments," Bess sighed and she shook her head to emphasize her displeasure. "Life is full of little adjustments. I suppose we'll all just have to bear down and get used to the changes for now. Things will get better I'm sure."

"I hope so," Cliff smiled and looked at Chet and Bess. "Well, you two have a good afternoon. I've got a hot poker game to get to."

Anita rolled her eyes at her husband's comment.

"Okay, Cliff," Chet said, shaking his neighbor's hand. "Enjoy the day, Mackleys."

On their way back to the Tranquil Tower's elevator, Chet and Bess reviewed what they liked about their meals. They discussed everything, from the cup of iced tea Bess drank to how the marinade for the chicken left an unpleasant taste in Chet's mouth. They also commented on their disdain for eating so early. Finally, they commented on the new found strategy to arrive early in the Dining Hall for meals.

Soon the elevator arrived and swept them up to the top floor. When the elevator doors opened, Bess and Chet lingered in front of a window in the hallway to admire the view. It was a scene of the Honey Hill's grounds that they never grew tired of. Full green grass spilled out in all directions, with trees lining the streets and independent living homes scattered around the property. Bess felt some sympathy for a groundskeeper she spotted cutting the grass.

"No one should have to work in this heat," Bess mumbled to herself, feeling some sympathy for the sweaty young man driving the lawnmower.

After commenting on the plight of the young man cutting the grass, Bess and Chet took a few steps down the hall and returned to their apartment. Once inside, Chet slipped into the bathroom to brush his teeth in hopes of washing away the taste of the marinade from his chicken.

"Maybe we should go for a short walk outside!" Chet called out from the bathroom.

"I feel full after that meal. We could walk to Dogwood Lane and check on the house."

"It'll be hot...but we can do that if you want to," Bess replied.

She stood by the large bay window and contemplated how hot they would get walking to Dogwood Lane in the early afternoon. While she didn't like to sweat, Bess thought, she would do it if it meant sneaking a peak at her house. Suddenly, a loud knock on the door interrupted her train of thought.

When Bess opened the door, she was surprised by what she found waiting on the other side. It was a face she didn't expect to see on her doorstep.

Chapter 5: MISSING

"Anita?" Bess asked, and she could feel her eyebrows drop down as they often did when she was surprised. "What are you doing here?"

"Hello, Bess," Anita said, her eyes glancing down nervously at her shoes. "Can I have a moment alone with you. I need to speak with you about an urgent matter."

"Well, Chet and I were just going to leave for a walk," Bess stated, gesturing to the door. "Would you like to join us? Chet will be right out and then we can go."

"No!" Anita quickly stated and the expression on her face conveyed a sense of desperation that her words and tone of voice did not. She took a step closer to Bess.

"Are you alright, Anita?" Bess asked.

"Like I said, I need to talk to you...in private," Anita spoke at barely above a whisper. "I have a delicate matter I need to share with you."

"We could have spoken in the Dining Hall," Bess suggested. "Why didn't you come over and sit with me?"

"What I have to tell you, Bess...it's a personal problem," Anita said and she leaned closer to Bess's ear. "There were too many people around in the Dining Hall to talk about it. Besides, I don't want your husband or mine to know what I'm about to tell you."

"Of course," Bess said.

The very moment she thought Anita would convey her concern, Chet emerged from the bedroom. He looked at Bess and Anita and stopped in his tracks. One thing Bess loved about her husband was that he had good instincts for people. In this instance, he could sense the awkwardness from the second he stepped into the room. When he looked at Anita the expression on her face told him something was wrong.

"Good morning, Anita," Chet smiled.

"Anita needs my help," Bess quietly stated.

Chet nodded and stepped closer to Bess.

"She looks upset," he whispered in her ear before giving her a quick kiss on the cheek. "Maybe you two should go for that walk. I have to write some notes for my Waltzing Club meeting. Go ahead, just tell me what the house looks like if they made any changes."

Chet gently squeezed Bess's hand before walking to the kitchen table, where he picked up a pen and paper and began to write on a small slip of paper. Bess smiled. She loved Chet for many reasons, but especially for his sense of understanding.

When Anita and Bess stepped outside, Bess could feel the heat quickly smother her in the face. It was like a warm damp blanket had been draped over her. The afternoon sun was bright and the sky was clear and blue like a sapphire. While the scene would look pretty from the windows in her apartment, she found the humid air stifling. She quickly felt her skin grow warm and sticky. She squinted at Anita who was leading her away from the main building and towards a garden.

"Let's sit in here for a minute and talk," Anita suggested, leading Bess to a small gazebo nestled beside a garden not far from the main building's entrance. Together they sat on a bench in the gazebo. Despite the shade, it was still very warm. A sympathetic breeze cast some temporary relief from the heat.

"Well…now we're alone," Bess sighed, wiping the sweat from her forehead. "There's a nice breeze blowing and it's just the two of us. What did you want to tell me, Anita?"

"I'm sorry for all this secrecy," Anita offered with a faint smile before shaking her head. "I'm sure you'd rather be back in your lovely apartment than out here. Your room looked nice from the few minutes I was inside. You and Chet really got lucky."

"It is a nice living arrangement," Bess replied. "I think we're the first ones to live there. Chet likes all the natural sunlight we get through the windows. I like the view of the grounds. Living on the top floor, I feel like a queen looking over her kingdom. Are you also in the Tranquil Tower?"

"No," Anita replied, "they put us near the chapel in a room smaller than yours. We hear lots of lovely organ music when there's a service. The nurses who check in on us seem very nice. They're always apologizing for the organ music but I told them we don't mind."

"The nurses here *are* helpful," Bess nodded. "I lived in the west wing of the main building for a little while before Chet and I got married and moved to Dogwood Lane. I had a very pleasant experience living there but I must admit…I'd rather be in my little home on Dogwood Lane."

"Me too," Anita sighed and she folded her hands on her lap and stared down at them. "Even though we've only been here for a short time, I still find my morning walks always lead me back to my house. There was this one morning when I even worked up the nerve to peek inside a window to see what work was being done."

"And what did you see?" Bess asked, her voice growing louder.

"Oh, Bess," Anita said, shaking her head. "It was terrible. There was such a mess. The whole scene just took my breath away. Ladders scattered around the rooms. Hardwood floors looking quite dirty. Empty paint cans scattered about. It really was quite shocking to see how much of a mess they made. Of course, that was a couple of days ago."

"Have you been back lately?" Bess asked. "I must admit that, with this heat wave, I haven't been going for my morning walks as often as I'd like."

"I walked back there yesterday," Anita sighed. "I told my husband that I forgot something at our house when we were packing. What he didn't know was that I took our house key along so I could check on something. It was something of great value that I kept hidden…even from my husband. So I let myself in just to check on my little secret."

Bess pressed her lips together and shook her head slightly.

"I don't think that was very wise," Bess said, feeling her eyebrows go down in a gesture to emphasize her concern. "You could have gotten caught, Anita. I know you received the same letter from the Honey Hills administration that I did. That letter was very clear about telling us to stay away from our homes while the renovations continued. If I recall, they even cited some legal issues for why they made the request. You're lucky those workers weren't around to report you."

"I know, I know" she said, waving her hand in front of Bess. "I was desperate, Bess. I simply had to look around and find something that means a great deal to me."

"And what was that?" Bess asked, pressing her concern. "What was so important, Anita, that you'd risk getting in trouble with the Honey Hills administration?"

"A dirty little secret from my past," Anita replied.

Those words caused Bess's mind to tune out the heat and the sweat forming on her face. She leaned in a little closer to Anita and locked on her eyes.

"What secret?" Bess asked.

Chapter 6: ANITA'S STORY

"In case I didn't mentioned it, Bess, I've never been lucky at love," Anita began, her eyes turning to some flowers planted in a garden near the gazebo where they were sitting. "I've been married quite a few times. When I was younger I married three times…and got divorced three times. In my fifties, I married for a fourth time but that dear husband died of a heart attack. So my current husband, Cliff, is my fifth go-round at marriage. We've been together for ten years now so I think I finally got it right."

"True love at last," Bess smiled.

Anita nodded at the comment while staring at the bright colors in the garden.

"Of course, with so many marriages and divorces in my life I have a few secrets," Anita continued. "Now my current husband, Cliff, is a good man. I love him very much and, like any good spouse, I want to help him avoid heartache. There are some things about my past that he simply doesn't need to know. One secret that I've never told him about is regarding my collection of ex-husbands….and wedding rings."

"Wedding rings?" Bess asked, instinctively glancing down at Anita's hand.

"Let me explain," Anita began, wiping some sweat from her forehead. "You see, I held onto all four of my wedding rings from my divorces. Counting the one Cliff gave me, that makes five diamond rings I own. Each ring means something special to me. I'm probably the only person in the Honey Hills Retirement community who can say they have five diamonds in their possession. That is…until four of them went missing this week."

Bess could feel her back grow straight after hearing those last four words.

"Excuse me?" Bess asked. "Did you say they're missing?"

"That's right," Anita nodded. "That's what I needed to tell you, Bess. You asked why I would take the risk of going into my house and getting in trouble? The day that bus drove us away it never occurred to me that I'd have to take my diamond rings along. After all, the letter said some workers were going to come and do simple tasks like lay carpet and paint a few walls. At least, that's what they told us in the letter they sent. Never in my wildest dreams did I imagine that someone would go through my personal effects and steal my diamond rings. You asked me earlier why I would risk getting into trouble to sneak back into my house? It was to check on those diamonds. In hindsight, I should have thought to take them with me when I left. Now…I'm afraid the thief has long since vanished."

This comment took Bess by surprise. She stopped staring at Anita and turned her eyes to some pink pansies just outside of the gazebo.

"So you think they were stolen…not misplaced?" Bess asked.

"With all the packing, and my granddaughter visiting, I simply forgot to take them along with me," Anita quickly replied. "You asked if I misplaced them? I know where I kept them every day since we came to the Honey Hills and moved into our home. Those diamonds aren't in that hiding place anymore."

Bess turned back to Anita and one question popped into her head.

"How do you know they were stolen?" Bess asked. "I mean, just because something is missing doesn't necessarily mean it was a crime."

"We've only been gone a couple of days," Anita stated. "Besides, I've seen the kind of people working in our neighborhood. In my opinion, they're dirty, uneducated and lacking in morals. If they're doing construction, in my opinion, they don't have a lot of money."

"A stereotype is always a convenient suspect," Bess mumbled to herself.

"What?" Anita asked.

"I said was there anything else missing?" Bess asked, trying to stay focused on the problem. "Any necklaces, bracelets or other items you can't account for?"

"Not that I've noticed," Anita quickly replied. "While I haven't had the time to look through everything, it appears that the rest of my jewelry is still where I left it. You see, that's the odd thing about this theft, Bess. My jewelry box is on my dresser...in plain sight...but nothing was taken from it. The rings were hidden under the box...and *they're* missing. How someone knew to ignore the jewelry in my box and look under the box...let's say I find that very curious."

"Did you ever call security and tell them what happened?" Bess asked.

"I can't really report this to the Honey Hills security or the police," Anita stated.

Bess waved her hand at a wayward fly buzzing around her eyes before focusing on Anita again.

"I don't understand," Bess said, feeling her eyebrows push together. "Your rings were stolen. You want them back. Why wouldn't you report this to security?"

"I'll tell you why," Anita began and she took a deep breath before speaking. "You see, I never really *told* Cliff that I held onto all of my other wedding rings. He's a very sensitive man and I don't want him to think I still harbor feelings for my ex-husbands. I've been divorced too many times, Bess. I don't want to risk it again."

"So why did you keep the rings?" Bess asked.

"Let's start with the obvious…they *are* diamonds," Anita replied in a very matter of fact tone of voice. "I chose to hold onto them for financial security not for sentiment. I know how quickly money can vanish in a divorce. Been down that road a few times. I thought if anything were to happen between me and Cliff I'd at least have those diamonds to help me survive. Not that Cliff would ever leave me but…."

"So you kept them for…financial security?" Bess asked again.

"Nothing more," Anita nodded.

Bess stood up and stepped out of the gazebo. The bright sunlight flashed in her eyes, causing her to squint. She turned and looked back to Anita, who was still seated in the shade of the gazebo. Despite the heat, Bess crossed her arms over her chest and considered what she was being asked to do.

"I don't know if I can help you," Bess finally stated in a clear direct tone of voice. "If you suspect one of the construction workers, there are quite a few of them. I'm not in a position to question every worker who comes into our neighborhood. As we both know, Anita, there is a heat wave going on this summer. I can't sit on my front porch for hours every day watching our neighborhood for suspicious workers. Maybe you just forgot where you put your rings. Maybe they're still in your house."

"That's the kind of condescending remark I'd expect to hear from a nurse!" Anita scolded, and for a moment Bess couldn't tell if it was Anita's emotions or the heat that was making her face turn red. "My memory is sharp as a tack, Bess. I know where I had those diamonds hidden and now they're gone. The construction workers are the only people who have had access to my home. The way I see it, they were the only ones with an opportunity to find my diamonds and take them. I'm just not sure what to do about it. If you won't help me…then what would you suggest?"

Bess wiped some beads of sweat from her face and became aware that the breeze was no longer blowing over her and Anita.

"Maybe I can find a clue or two," she quickly suggested. "Let's start with your house. Can you take me there, Anita? I want to see exactly where you hid those precious diamonds. If I can see the room and the hiding place…maybe something will click."

"I can do that," Anita answered before quickly standing up and stepping out of the gazebo.

Bess looked at the sweat glistening on her forearms. She felt sticky and hot and glanced over at the main building and thought briefly about stepping inside. The cool air conditioning was tempting to consider, but the look of desperation on Anita's face told Bess she was destined for a hot walk down to the scene of the crime.

Chapter 7 : BACK TO DOGWOOD LANE

Once they left the shade of the gazebo and headed for Dogwood Lane, Bess couldn't help but notice that she and Anita were the only two residents who were brave enough, or crazy enough, to be out on such a hot summer day.

The sky was clear, the sun burned brightly and Bess was beginning to feel like a piece of toast. While her head was being struck from above by the sun, her legs could feel the heat being cast up from the black top road they walked down. On occasion, they'd pass under the shade of a tree where they'd linger for a moment to cool off as best they could. The afternoon temperature reinforced Bess's belief that a morning walk was more agreeable when done early.

Soon they reached Dogwood Lane, at which point Bess let her mind grow silent, her eyes grow wide and she felt her heart swoon at the sight of her beloved home. Instinctively she began to walk up her driveway when she felt someone grab her by the arm.

"Be careful," Anita advised, letting go of Bess's wrist. "There are workers at the house next to yours, Bess. They might even be in your house. They wouldn't be happy too happy if you walked in while they were working."

She knew what Anita said was true. Her heart wanted to ignore Anita's warning and glimpse at the changes in her home. However, Bess knew the advice was sound.

'I suppose you're right," Bess sighed.

"I don't see any activity on my side of the street," Anita observed. "Wait here and let me look through the windows to see if anyone's inside"

While she waited for Anita to walk up her driveway to check for workers, Bess looked back across the street at her own home. The windows, the roof, the front door all looked like nothing had been changed. The front lawn was well-manicured. The shrubs perfectly trimmed. Her eyes locked on the chair on her front porch and it seemed to be willing her to stroll over and sit down. It took every fiber in her body not to run over and step back into her home and reclaim her old way of life.

She turned to the home next door where some trucks were parked. She saw all kinds of equipment scattered randomly around the front lawn. The scene looked like a construction truck simply belched everything out on the grass, Bess thought. She turned back to Anita, who was just stepping away from her front porch. She quickly cut through the yard and looked at Bess. When she got closer, Bess spotted a silly grin on Anita's face.

"I think we're safe," Anita gleefully reported. "I don't see anyone in my house. We'd better move quickly, though, before we get spotted by a worker."

"Lead the way," Bess replied.

Together they quickly walked up the driveway, but didn't head for the porch. Instead Bess followed Anita to the side of her garage. Anita led her along the side of the garage where they stopped in front of a side door. Bess watched Anita reach down and grab a small metal bucket on the ground next to the door. Anita picked up the bucket, turned it upside down and a key dropped into her hand. She slipped the key into the lock, opened the door, then turned her head one more time to see if anyone was watching them.

"Follow me," Anita whispered, cracking the door open and stepping inside.

Bess looked over her shoulder one time before following Anita inside.

They stepped through the doorway and into the garage. The moment they set foot in the garage, Bess quickly noticed that it was empty. Like many residents in the Honey Hills' community, it appeared that Anita and her husband used the space for storage rather than a car. Bess felt a bit sympathetic for Anita and her husband. Since they didn't own a car there were no opportunities for them to escape the Honey Hills Community. She felt fortunate that Chet still owned his car and that they used it on occasion to drive into town for some groceries or a meal.

Together Anita and Bess made their way through the dim interior of the garage. Daylight sprayed in through a small window, offering strands of pale light for Bess to view her surroundings. In one corner, she spotted some gardening tools and a small bag of potting soil. Along a far wall she spied what appeared to be a silhouette of a work bench. She also noticed some boxes stacked in a corner. Fumbling around the dark was not something Bess enjoyed doing, but she did her best out of sympathy for Anita's plight.

"I found the door," Anita's voice announced.

Suddenly, Bess saw a door crack open and light filled her view. She followed Anita inside and quickly recognized that they were finally entering the house. The first room they stepped into looked familiar.

"Our garage also leads into the kitchen," Bess stated, following Anita inside.

Anita grew silent, allowing her eyes to take in the details around her.

"This is a welcome sight," she sighed, standing in the middle of her kitchen. She reached out with one hand and stroked her toaster the way someone might pet a dog. "Oh, how I've missed my kitchen, Bess. I love to cook. You can only imagine how badly I'm coping with having someone else make my meals."

Anita lingered by the refrigerator, smiling at it like it was a long-lost friend. She took a few more steps, making eye contact with every cupboard and shelf. She did one final walk around the kitchen, her fingers brushing over appliances like they were wayward children.

"So nice to see," she smiled.

Finally, she led Bess out of the kitchen and into the living room. She followed behind Anita, then accidently bumped into her. For some reason, Anita had abruptly stopped in the middle of the room. After excusing herself for the collision, Bess saw the reason why Anita came to a standstill. She was staring at a cloth tarp that held paint cans. Bess looked around to see more tarps and more paint cans scattered throughout the sitting room. At the center of the room she spotted a six foot ladder. Anita turned to Bess and shook her head.

"My children were never this messy," Anita remarked, placing her hands on her hips and casting a look of disdain at the sight. "Don't you think they should at least clean up before they leave? Tools on my dining room table, a tarp on my carpeting. It'll take me weeks to clean up."

"I don't think you'll have to lift a finger," Bess pointed out. "I'm sure when they're finished they will leave all of our homes as good as new."

"I hope so," Anita sighed and she shook her head. "This is just…horrendous."

"We didn't come here to just look at the chaos," Bess observed. "Can you show me to your bedroom? I want to see where you hid your rings."

Both ladies carefully stepped over a drop cloth and turned down a narrow hallway leading to the bedroom. With thoughts of tarps and empty paint cans swirling in her head, Bess couldn't help but wonder what her home might look like. Were the walls painted or scraped? Were the drapes up or down? Was there dirt on the rug? Was there just as much disorder?

When she entered the bedroom, Bess could sense Anita's relief to find the room was neat as a pin. There wasn't a tool to be had or a dirty tarp to be found. Bess walked around, noticing the color of choice in the room. The flamingo pink bedspread, the pictures on the wall framed with the same tone of pink, and even the color of the curtains matched the color of the pink frames.

"You certainly have a bright theme in this room," Bess commented.

"I do," Anita grinned. "It gets my motor going when I wake up in the morning. Cliff is very understanding about my choices in bright colors. Fortunately for me, it appears they aren't making any changes to the color scheme in my bedroom."

"If nothing has been painted or changed," Bess began, her eyes scanning the room, "wouldn't it be safe to conclude that no work has been done in here?"

"I...I guess," Anita nodded, "but they *were* in my house."

"I understand," Bess continued, "but if no one worked in your bedroom then I suspect it's safe to conclude that no workers were in here to look for you diamonds. Where did you keep them, Anita?"

Anita grew silent and her eyes danced around the walls while she absorbed this statement.

"Let me show you, Bess," Anita finally stated. She stepped over to her dresser and stopped in front of the mirror. She picked up a small wooden box from the dresser and carried it over to Bess. The box was packed with a wide array of pins, necklaces, earrings and bracelets.

"This is it," she said, handing Bess the box. "This is where I kept my diamonds and the rest of my jewelry."

Bess scooped up the box with both hands and was surprised at how heavy it was. She glanced down at the jewelry that was nearly spilling out the top of the box. While there was no apparent organization, it was quite apparent to Bess that Anita loved jewelry. In fact, she probably could use a second jewelry box.

"So you went through all of these items *before* you realized you were missing your rings?" Bess asked, poking at the pile of jewelry with one finger.

"The thief didn't have to dig through all this jewelry to find my diamonds," Anita answered before grabbing the box from Bess and dumping out the contents onto her bed.

"What are you doing?" Bess asked, stepping closer to the bed.

"Look here," Anita instructed.

She flipped the box upside down and pointed at a narrow piece of masking tape stuck to the underside of the box. Bess took the jewelry box from Anita and held the box close to her face.

"What's this for?" Bess asked, her eyes moving from the pile on the bed to the masking tape on the box. "Is your box cracking?"

"That's where I hid them," Anita explained, pointing at the tape.

"Your diamond rings?" Bess asked.

"That's right," Anita replied. "I kept them taped to the underside of my jewelry box."

Bess turned her eyes back to the box she was holding. The size of the box was small, barely noticeable to Bess when she first entered the room. Yet, Bess thought, someone knew enough to walk over to Anita's dresser, ignore the pile of jewelry stuffed in the box, and turn the container over to remove the rings from under the tape. Despite Anita's suspicions, Bess knew this was a detail that no carpenter or painter would simply stumble across. The location of those rings was a more intimate detail that, she suspected, only a small number of people would know about.

"You said you kept the rings a secret from Cliff?" Bess asked.

"That's right," Anita replied, scooping the jewelry back into her box.

"So he wouldn't have even known where to look," Bess mumbled to herself. "Was there anyone else who knew about your diamond rings?"

"When you've been married as many times as I have, a surplus of failed marriages really doesn't come up in casual conversations," Anita stated. "So, no, I can't think of anyone I would have told about my rings. Being married so many times…it's just not something I like to brag about in social circles."

"I see," Bess said, watching Anita finish putting her jewelry away. Bess walked around the room, silently scanning the walls, the furniture and the rug one more time. Her eyes locked on one nightstand next to the bed that contained a framed photo of a young man holding a little girl dressed like a princess. The girl appeared to be no older than five, with sky blue eyes, curly dark hair and a smile that was as cute as a button. Bess turned, pointed at the picture and grinned. "Who is this adorable young lady wearing the crown?"

"That's my son and my granddaughter," Anita smiled. "I keep them on my nightstand so when I wake up in the morning the first thing I see is their smiles. They're my sunshine."

"Grandchildren make a difference," Bess nodded. "I have a granddaughter who is sweeter than pie. I love when she visits me. And I just learned I'm going to have another grandchild soon."

"That's wonderful news, Bess," Anita smiled. "I think grandchildren light up the darkest days. I love when my granddaughter comes by to visit me. As you might guess, she loves dressing up like a princess...or so I recall."

"What do you mean?" Bess asked.

"My son and granddaughter haven't been around to visit as much as they used to," she reported.

"Really?" Bess asked, stepping closer. "Why did they stop coming to see you?"

"It's not a family spat or anything like that," Anita answered, her voice dropping as if she were embarrassed by this fact. "My son has been out of work. So he's been very busy calling potential employers. He tells me he's always going on interviews. From what I understand it's very difficult to find a job these days."

"Does he have any prospects?" Bess asked.

"Not yet," Anita replied, her eyes turning back to the photo. "I talk to him every day, and he's always on his way to one interview or setting up another. He's a real go-getter."

"I think that's a quality any employer would value," Bess smiled. "I'd imagine you say a prayer for him every night to help him find a job."

"While I appreciate your concern for my son, can we get back to talking about my rings?" Anita asked and she sat down on the bed facing her dresser. "I want to know how you'll solve this mystery, Bess. What suspects will you focus on? Maybe we should spy on the workers right now. I noticed a few of them working on a home across the street. Maybe we should leave my house and go over there and see what they're up to. Listen to what they talk about."

"I don't think that will be necessary," Bess smiled.

"Maybe we should be more direct," Anita suggested. "Perhaps we should just walk through the front door and confront them about my missing diamond rings. If we're lucky maybe one of them will confess."

"Oh, Anita," Bess laughed. "I'm not good at those kind of confrontations. As much as I know you want those rings back…I'm afraid I just can't walk up to a stranger, scream an accusation and solve a mystery in five minutes. I need some time to let my thoughts and observations percolate."

"I understand," Anita nodded and her eyes drifted back to the jewelry box. "Everything in its own time. That's what my mother would say."

"Wise words," Bess said.

After checking a few more rooms, and commenting on the mess in the living room one more time, Anita finally led Bess out of her house and down to Dogwood Lane. As they headed back to the main building, Bess turned her eyes to the side of the street. Dogwood Lane was quieter than usual. It seemed strange to Bess not to see anyone sitting on a porch, or working in a garden, or walking along the street. She glimpsed over at her own home which still appeared to have no workers inside.

"Would you excuse me, Anita," Bess said, cutting to the other side of the street. "I just want to go over and check on my gardens. Would you care to join me? I have some lovely things growing back there that need my attention. Would you like to see what flowers I've grown?"

"I'm sorry, Bess, but it's too hot to look at flowers," Anita replied, fanning her face with her hand. "I'm going to walk back to the main building as fast as I can and get back in the air conditioning. You should do the same."

"Suit yourself," she smiled.

Bess crossed the street and headed up the driveway to her home, thinking about how much her gardens had changed. The closer she got the more she could feel her cheeks rise above a broad smile. When she caught a glimpse of her gardens, the bright sunshine and warm air magically became more tolerable. Happiness seemed to take away the oppressive heat.

Out of the corner of her eye she saw the back porch and the two chairs where she and Chet would sit in the evenings to watch the sunset. Towards the back of the yard, Bess found her precious gardens.

As she did the previous summer, Bess designated one of her gardens for vegetables and the other one for flowers. She carefully walked around each garden, examining what was thriving and what was struggling. Eventually, she went back to the porch to retrieve her garden hose. She turned on the water and pulled the hose out to the gardens. She stopped between the two gardens and began to spray everything she could see.

"Time to do your happy dance," Bess whispered, as she watched her plants wiggling and moving under the cascading water.

While the air was sprinkled with the sounds of workers hammering, using power saws, and calling to each other, Bess was oblivious to the noise. She was happily focused on her gardens.

She smiled at the lush green growth that filled her eyes. On occasion, she'd bend down and pull a weed or two. Brushing some dirt from her hands, she looked around. For a moment, she felt like she was back in the comforts of her old life. She felt like she was back in the carefree routine she missed. Standing next to her gardens, she felt like her heart was home.

Chapter 8: CARDS AND ADVICE

While she shuffled a deck of cards to open another meeting of Bridge Club, Bess let her eyes linger on the three familiar faces sitting around the table. She knew that any resident of the Honey Hills Center was welcome to attend their Bridge Club, but Bess and her friends took a low-key approach to advertising their group. Over the years Bess, Rose, Flo and Alma enjoyed each other's company. Perhaps that was why they were so hesitant to invite new people. As a group, they had good chemistry and didn't want that balance to be tipped.

While Bess dealt the cards, she couldn't help but sense the silence around her. It was unusual for her friends to be so quiet this early in the morning. A meeting of the Bridge Club was typically a place where gossip and small talk were freely exchanged over cards. So after the first round of bridge quietly drew to a close Bess decided to address the silence.

"Is there something wrong?" she asked.

"Nothing that I know of," Rose observed.

"Why are you all so...quiet this morning?" Bess asked.

"I was just going to ask you the same thing, Bess," Rose grinned.

"So was I," Alma added. "Are you really that miserable living here, Bess? I mean, you haven't smiled once since you arrived this morning. I know this isn't Dogwood Lane, but you don't have to look so glum about your circumstances. Things around here aren't *that* bad. You'll be back in that lovely little home in no time."

"I'm not sad," Bess said, turning her eyes to the cards she was holding. "It's not that. I'm just…preoccupied with my thoughts."

"Thoughts about what?" Alma asked.

"I was just talking to one of my neighbors yesterday," Bess explained. "Her name is Anita Mackley. You see, Anita lives across the street from me on Dogwood Lane. Like me, she and her husband were temporarily moved here because of the ongoing renovations. Unfortunately for Anita, she made a terrible discovery. It seems that some of her jewelry has vanished from her home. Now she suspects the workers of the theft."

"What sort of jewelry?" Rose asked.

"Four diamond rings," Bess replied. "The day she left her home they were safely hidden and then…those four diamonds simply vanished like steam from a tea pot."

"My goodness," Rose said, covering her mouth with her hand.

"Now that sounds interesting!" Alma grinned, her voice growing louder and her back growing straighter in her chair. "We should have been talking about this all morning. Tell us more, Bess."

"Anita took me inside her house yesterday to show me where she kept her diamonds hidden and I must admit…they were not kept in an obvious place. They really would have been hard to find. While the idea of stolen diamonds is shocking, I was also stunned by what I saw in Anita's home. Specifically, the level of mess left by the workers renovating her home," Bess sighed.

"What kind of mess?" Rose asked.

"It was quite a scene," Bess continued. "Tarps here, paint cans there, tools scattered everywhere. After what I saw in Anita's house, I must admit I'm afraid to look through the windows of my own home. Who knows what I'll find. I just keep envisioning those workers trampling through *my* house, painting rooms in some awful color and changing things for the worse. It really is a helpless feeling to know that someone can refashion the place where you live without even asking for your input. I love my house. I hope I recognize it the day they let me back inside. I often wonder why they even decided to start fixing up our homes."

"It's because retirement is a business," Rose replied with a blunt tone of voice.

"Pardon?" Bess asked, lost in her thoughts.

"She said retirement is *all* business!" Flo spoke a little louder.

"Why would you say that?' Bess asked, glancing at Flo and then Rose.

"I'm merely repeating what I overheard," Rose said.

"From whom?" Bess asked.

"Not so long ago I eavesdropped on two nurses talking about this very thing," Rose began, lowering her cards. "You see, they described all the changes being made by the owners of the Honey Hills while they were filling out some charts at their station. At first, they said the changes were small and subtle. They started by replacing the street signs with new ones. Adding new gardens. Even changing the color of the siding on some buildings. Then they built those new Tranquil Tower apartments where you and Chet are staying. They even did some renovations here in the main building. The goal, or so I overheard, is to change the actual appearance of the Honey Hills retirement community.

Once all the changes are made they plan to make the biggest change of all."

"And what would that be?" Bess asked.

Rose paused and made eye contact with each person at the table.

"Renaming our retirement community," Rose stated.

"Rename it?" Alma gasped.

"You mean it won't be called *Honey Hills* anymore?" Bess asked.

"I'm afraid not," Rose sighed. "From what I've overheard, no name has been chosen yet but it's only a matter of time."

"Why on earth would they do that?" Bess asked.

"In making all these changes," Rose explained, "and in changing the Honey Hills name, the owners hope that by rebranding our lovely retirement community it will attract more retirees to live here."

"More people?" Alma asked.

"Is that really necessary?" Bess chimed in. "I think we have plenty of residents living here and in the independent living homes on the grounds."

"Not necessarily," Rose commented. "Since you moved to Dogwood Lane, Bess, the numbers are down. I've been living here longer than any of you. When I walk around the halls I see lots of vacant rooms. Fewer people to sit and chat with. I wasn't sure why they were building a new apartment tower if the numbers were down. After what I overheard from those nurses…now I understand."

"It would be so sad to know this place by any other name," Alma sighed.

Everyone grew silent as they quietly absorbed the fate of their retirement home.

"Are we going to play cards now?" Flo finally spoke up. "I enjoy a little chit-chat but I want to win a few rounds of cards too. Can we stop flapping our gums, ladies?"

"Wait a minute, Flo," Rose mumbled.

"You're so insensitive!" Alma snapped with a sarcastic tone and her eyes locked on Flo. "Don't you care about what happens around here? Don't you care that they're changing our retirement home?"

"I don't care if they rename this place the Honey Bee Hive!" Flo grumbled and then she paused and pointed around the table. "What should matter to all of you is that whatever name they call this place...we still have a home. We still get our meals. We still have a roof over our heads. We still have each other. For me, all I need is a room and a bed. The other stuff doesn't matter."

It was one of those rare instances, Bess thought, *where Flo Morgenstern got in the last word on the topic*. Her thought was so succinct and so direct that it cut right to the core of the matter. No one had anything else to say on the topic. They looked at each other and quietly began to play the cards they were dealt.

In a few hours, Bridge Club was over and all parties went their separate ways. Bess walked back to the Tranquil Tower where she took the elevator up to her room. When the elevator stopped at the top floor, Bess stepped out. She wandered down a long hallway and paused by a window that overlooked the countryside. She stepped up to the window and let her eyes take in the scenery.

"Always a pretty sight," she sighed.

Laid out before her was a view of a farmer's field. It was lush and green and appeared to run right up to the horizon where it met a pure blue sky. Even though she'd lingered by this window many times since moving, the view always demanded her attention. Every time she took in the scenery she'd spot a new detail.

Judging by the dark green appearance of the crop, Bess guessed that it was some kind of soybeans. When a gust of wind blew just right, Bess also noticed how it caused a ripple to push through the bean field. She watched a few more gusts of wind brush over the plants and she couldn't help but let out a sigh at the beauty of it all.

"Like an emerald ocean," Bess whispered to herself.

It was such a calming scene she could feel her thoughts about the missing diamonds melt away. Her moment of tranquility was interrupted by a curious sight. Her eyes were drawn to something just off to the side of the field.

Standing next to the bean field, beneath a brutally warm sun, Bess spotted a woman at the edge of the field. Her back was to Bess, which made it difficult to identify her. She wore a canary yellow dress, had a full head of bluish-white hair that fell around her shoulders. She did not appear to be going anywhere. In fact, she stood perfectly still.

"She must be sweltering out there," Bess quietly observed.

She couldn't make out who or what the woman was looking at but, in her opinion, it was clearly too hot to be standing outside to admire a farmer's field. In fact, Bess reasoned, the woman could easily appreciate the same view from inside the main building. She remained by the window for a good five minutes, staring at the field and glancing back at the woman. Finally, Bess gave voice to one question lingering in her head.

"What could she possibly find that interesting out there?"

It was the kind of scene that might not warrant the attention of other people. It was a simple sight, a woman standing by a field. It wouldn't cause a car to stop or a jogger to break stride. Yet, for Bess, the fact that this woman was standing outside, in the middle of a blistering hot day, staring as if she were in some kind of trance was a curiosity. It gave Bess something to ponder for the rest of the day.

Chapter 9: DILEMMA OVER BREAKFAST

A week went by and Bess gave barely a second thought to the woman she saw by the field. There were no more sightings and Bess lost interest in the woman's motives.

Instead, she was now giving a good deal of thought to Anita and her missing wedding rings. No matter how many times she went over it in her head, Bess felt stuck. It was like having writer's block, but for a detective. The suspects that Anita accused were always outside in the heat, always busy working, and always keeping to themselves. It made it challenging for Bess to observe them, given the triple digit temperatures. In short, Bess was starting to feel a mild sense of panic over not being able to identify a suspect.

During her morning walks to Dogwood Lane, she actually began to hide behind trees or peak inside windows of other homes to watch what few workers arrived early to work. She saw a few of them doing plenty of painting, hammering, cutting of wood and laying of new rugs. They were all business, with little talking or checking their phones. They were clearly focused when they worked, which is what Bess was not hoping to find. She didn't see one person snooping around a home or sneaking around.

From all of her observations, and a few encounters with the workers, she concluded that the young men and women assigned to work on Dogwood Lane were a polite, friendly and hard-working bunch. All in all, Bess found nothing in what they did or said to question their character or motives. However, she did manage to learn a few interesting things from those sweaty morning walks.

One morning she managed to speak to a few of the workers who told her that the company doing the renovations was a family owned business. It was owned by a father and two sons who ran a tight ship. Another morning she actually peeked in through a house window, where she saw an Amish man installing a kitchen cabinet. It was not all that unusual to see Amish men working on a construction site in this part of Pennsylvania. A final observation came from one crew member who revealed he was actually splitting time between the renovations on Dogwood Lane and two other building sites that the company was operating. This bit of news told Bess that the company was thriving, which also meant the workers had steady jobs and steady income. All clues worth noting, Bess thought, but none of them pointing her to a suspect.

One afternoon she was enjoying her air-conditioned apartment, thinking about the possible suspects for stealing Anita's diamonds. Her thoughts were interrupted by a phone call.

"Hello," a voice said on the other end of the phone. "My name is Tom Gordon. Is this Bess Bullock?"

"It is," she replied.

"I have a problem," Tom said. "Well, maybe not as much a problem as...a curiosity. I was wondering if you had some time to meet with me tomorrow morning?"

"Meet?" Bess asked. "I don't even know you. What's this in regards to?"

"As I said, I have a curious problem I'd like you to look into for me," Tom explained. "Do you know where those small tennis courts are located? The ones beside the main building?"

"I know where you mean. I pass those courts on my morning walks. I've often wondered why they made those tennis courts so small," Bess replied.

"Well, they look like tennis courts, but that's not what they're used for," Tom stated. "At any rate, I was wondering if you'd be willing to meet me there tomorrow morning?"

"Why?" Bess inquired.

"Like I said, I have a little mystery I'd like you to solve," he replied. "Now I've been told you're the one to call about such matters here at the Honey Hills. Someone from your Bridge Club told me that. If that isn't the case then forget about this phone call and I'll handle it myself."

Not too many people knew about Bridge Club, which told Bess there was some truth to what this man was saying. She was struck by the comment and was intrigued that one of her friends would recommend her to help a fellow resident.

"No, no," Bess commented. "I do like a good mystery. Can you give me some specifics? I'll warn you, I don't know a lot about sports, if that's what this is about."

"It's not a sports mystery," the man's voice quickly answered. "It has more to do with the behavior of a friend and his...morning routine."

Curious about such a statement, she quickly accepted the invitation and decided to brave the heat again to meet Tom Gordon.

The following morning, while Bess got dressed, she instantly became aware of a problem. The moment she heard Chet remind her that it was time for breakfast in the Dining Hall, she quickly realized she was double-booked. She explained the scheduling dilemma involving Mr. Gorman, kissed Chet on the cheek and asked him to bring her back a blueberry muffin. Together they took the elevator down. She walked with Chet to the Dining Hall and left him at a table by himself. The sight of pancakes on a nearby table left her stomach growling in objection to not being fed. She ignored her hunger pangs and left the Dining Hall. Once she found the main doors, she stepped outside and began her walk to the small tennis courts.

"One simple phone call," Bess complained to herself as she walked along Magnolia Lane. "One simple phone call and here I am, in the heat, sweating and hungry. Why don't I just say "no" to people?"

It was a question she pondered for the rest of her walk. When she arrived at the small tennis courts she quieted her complaints out of respect for the men playing on the court. They were engaged in some kind of game. She stood next to the court and began to notice, as Tom Gordon told her, that the game they were playing wasn't tennis.

She settled into a comfy red Adirondack chair, trying to ignore the late morning sun as it blazed in the sky, and watched the activity on the court. Her chair was fixed in the grass next to the small tennis courts where she had a good view. She noticed how the men were paired off, with two on one side of the court and two on the other. They each held a wooden paddle that they swung at a small plastic ball. Once one of them hit the ball, it went over a net at the center of the court to another pair of men who chased it down and tried to hit it back. It looked like tennis, Bess thought, but it was clearly a different version of the sport.

In between the sounds of a plastic ball hitting wooden paddles, there were also bursts of laughter and conversation from the men. Like her Bridge Club, it was clear to Bess that all four men were having as much fun talking to each other as they were playing their game. With so much good sportsmanship and laughter in the air, Bess began to wonder why she had been invited to the court.

"What mystery could there possibly be about four friends having fun?" Bess quietly asked herself. As the points came and went she could feel the temperature rising. She also began to question the wisdom of her decision. Why did she agree to come out at this late hour?

She took a deep breath and tried to ignore the late morning sunshine. She wiped away a thin layer of sweat building on her forehead and squinted at the players. She was amazed at how the men didn't seem to mind the warm conditions. How they were able to run and swing with such vigor. Judging by their smiles and occasional laughter, it appeared they didn't even know it was going to be another day near one hundred degrees.

"For heaven's sake, why am I out here?" Bess complained to herself.

She was surprised to see the tallest man on the court turn his head in her direction.

"Wait a minute…we're almost done!" he called over to her.

"Okay," Bess smiled.

She was embarrassed that she had complained so loudly. A few minutes went by and Bess found herself confused by the game she was watching. All four men had white hair and wore white short sleeved shirts with matching shorts. They tried their best to negotiate around the court with their thin legs and teetering strides. Two of the men wore knee braces on their legs while the other two had stomachs so large they appeared to have pillows tucked under their shirts.

Despite their knee braces and round stomachs, all four men ran and played with great enthusiasm.

Soon she found her eyes darting around at the action while she tried to figure out the rules. They all took good healthy swings at the ball and were clearly enjoying themselves. After a few minutes, Bess came to the realization that while her sharp mind was adept at reading people, it wasn't as sharp interpreting the rules of this game.

Finally, one shot went into the net and judging by the reaction of all four men, Bess sensed that their contest was over. The four men walked to the net, shook hands, and began to leave the court. Spotting an opportunity to introduce herself, she stepped closer to the court watching the men gather their things and, one by one, begin to leave the court. She smiled and nodded as each man stepped off the court and walked by her. They all appeared to be lathered in sweat and smelling awful.

"You looking for an autograph?" one man chuckled.

"No," Bess quietly answered, trying to ignore the smell trailing off each player.

"She's here for me!" another man's voice called out.

Bess looked to find the tallest man of the group making eye contact with her. He smiled and wiped the back of his neck with a towel. He was tall, wore glasses, had a white beard and a knee brace on his right knee. Bess could only guess that this was the man she spoke to on the phone. This was the man who'd lured her away from her air-conditioned apartment to come out on this steamy summer morning.

"Are you Tom Gordon?" she asked.

The question caused one of the other players to laugh at her.

"What's this, Tom?" he called out, dangling a thumb in Bess's direction. "You got yourself a girlfriend?"

"Girlfriend?" Tom quickly shot back. "Last time I heard a question like that I must've been in high school!"

"Don't worry, Tom," the man laughed, "I won't tell your wife!"

Bess could feel her face grow flushed. This time she knew her face was red but it wasn't from the heat. She couldn't hide her embarrassment over being the subject of such a silly conversation. She looked down to avoid eye contact and stepped onto the court where Tom Gordon was waiting. She glanced over her shoulder at the other three men lingering just outside the fence. They were silent and grinning at her, which made her feel like the self-conscious girl she used to be in high school.

"I'll catch up with you, fellas!" Tom said, waving his hand for them to leave. "Go ahead and get some drinks. I'll catch up."

With those words, Bess watched the other three players turn and make their way back into the main building. She heard them talking about air conditioning, cold drinks and a desire to escape the heat. Bess squinted up at the sun and tried not to think about the perspiration on her face when she turned back to the man who invited her.

"So, Mr. Gordon," she began, mustering a smile through the heat, "this looks like quite a fun sport. You and your friends really sound like you were having a good time out there...in spite of these hot conditions. What do you call the game you were playing?"

"It's called pickleball," Tom replied and he stroked his white beard for good measure. "I like to say...it's the sport that old tennis players play after they die."

"What do you mean...*after* they die?" Bess asked.

"I mean that tennis players, like myself, devote our lives to the sport," he began. "We join tennis leagues.

We play in tennis tournaments. Then one day old age comes along and takes away our wheels."

He pointed down to a knee brace on his leg.

"You know what it's like when your brain wants to keep competing but your knees and hips refuse to listen to reason?" he asked.

"No," Bess sighed.

"Well…it ain't a pleasant experience," he answered. "Any orthopedic doctor would tell you as much."

Bess wiped some more sweat from her face and forced a smile.

"Aging is seldom fun," she quietly observed.

"This game of pickleball takes some of the sting out of it for me," Tom observed. "At my age, it's still fun to get together with the boys and play in the morning. We all enjoy a little competition and we don't have to run that much. Of course, these days we gotta play early before it gets too hot. This summer is one of the hottest on record, or so the weatherman likes to say, Mrs. Bullock."

"I think he's right, Mr. Gordon," Bess nodded, wiping some more perspiration from her forehead. "I was getting hot just sitting there watching you play. When I go for walks, I'm usually out much earlier in the morning. So now that I'm covered in sweat, can you tell me why you asked me to come out here? And…how do you know my name? I think this is the first time we've ever met."

"You're right," Gordon laughed and he wiped his face with a small towel. "There are lots of people living here at the Honey Hills and it's hard to meet everyone. As it turns out we actually have a mutual friend who thinks very highly of you."

"And who is that?" she asked.

"Flo Morgenstern," he stated. "I believe you know her from playing cards?"

"Oh, yes," Bess nodded, "we've been friends for many years."

"Well, she and I have a mutual love for competition," he stated with a vacant smile and nod. "When we sit together for bingo night, Flo is ruthless. She doesn't' like to lose at anything. She pounds the table with her fist and mumbles some mean words. She's very passionate about winning."

"That's a good observation," Bess smiled. "For as long as I've known her, all Flo cares about is winning at cards and bingo. Flo doesn't care about juicy gossip or idle chatter. She cares about winning."

"Now, of course, I'm different than Flo," he explained. "I don't need to win at *everything*. I just enjoy competing against other people. That's why I'm asking for your help, Mrs. Bullock. You see, I've been playing with the same fellas for about a year now. As you saw this morning, we all have a good time. However, things have started to change this last month. Out here on the pickleball court, good competition has been a problem. In fact, it's been very…inconsistent. One of our own is to blame."

"I don't understand," Bess confessed. "Blame…for what?"

"For wasting my time," Tom Gordon replied.

Bess felt her eyebrows lower and asked Mr. Gordon to tell her more.

Chapter 10: THE CURIOUS PICKLEBALL PLAYER

"I remember the day I first moved to the Honey Hills Center," Tom Gordon recalled. "The day I unpacked my last box, I looked out the window to my new room and saw this court for the first time. It was an unexpected surprise to see a pickleball court here at the Honey Hills. I was thrilled because I knew I could keep playing the sport I loved."

"How nice for you," Bess smiled.

"Over the next few weeks I started to make friends, as most people do when they move to a retirement home," Tom continued. "Within a week of moving here, I began to put out feelers for residents who also played pickleball. When my wife died, I moved here in the early winter so I had some time to mingle, socialize and get to know other residents. I started to find some pickleball players. By spring, I had met three pretty good friends who liked pickleball. Like me, they were all former tennis players who took up the sport because their knees and hips were too bad to run. With such similar experiences, and the same sense of humor, we all really got along the first time we met each other. It was a good sign."

"How lucky for you," Bess nodded.

"Come spring time," Tom continued, "we all decided to get together on a weekly basis. From the first few mornings we played it was clear that our personalities and passions were perfectly aligned."

"How so?" Bess asked.

"Take the first morning we played pickleball," he recollected. "That first time there was never one angry word spoken. I think we must have played for two hours that morning. When we were done, we stayed out on the court and talked for another hour. We were like brothers when we left that court. For the rest of that spring and summer, we all enjoyed our Thursday morning pickleball matches. Later in the year when winter arrived, we managed to stay in touch."

"How?" she asked.

"We'd stop by each other's rooms," Tom recalled. "Sometimes we'd sit together after lunch and chat and catch up. By the time spring rolled around again we were back out on the court. That first month...things went really well. It felt good to be playing pickleball again. Then...heading into this summer... our foursome began to take a downward turn."

"What happened?" Bess asked. "Did someone get sick?"

"No," Tom replied. "You see there's this one player in our group. His name is Mack McCall. Now old Mack is a nice enough fella. He's a little wide around the waist. You might remember him cuz he's heavier than the rest of the fellas."

"I think I know who you mean," Bess nodded.

"Anyway," he continued, "there were some mornings when Mack would come right on time and when that happened he'd play lights out pickleball. Those were good mornings and everyone would have fun. Then there were other mornings when Mack would sleep late and we'd have to wait for him. When he'd finally arrive, Mack would be way off his game. He'd have a terrible time hitting the ball. As a matter of fact, it just happened again last week. This morning he came right on time. Me and the other fellas know that when it's a morning that Mack is running late for pickleball, he's gonna be struggling to play well. Lately, it's been happening more frequently. Some of the fellas are getting frustrated and want to find a person to replace Mack. They're tired of him coming late and ruining the morning for the rest of us by playing badly. We all just want to compete and have fun."

"Do you also want Mack out of the group?" Bess asked.

"I like Mack," he replied. "I know I'm not out here to win a trophy. I'm here to spend time with friends, so no, I don't agree with them. Mack's friendship comes before winning for me. If he's having a bad morning…I'm okay with that."

"So what do you want me to do?" Bess asked.

"I know occasionally sleeping late does us all a world of good," Tom explained, "but I have to believe that there's more going on with Mack. Something besides a bad alarm clock. Something that I'm hoping could be fixed so he can continue on with us."

"Like what?" Bess asked.

"At our age, it could be many things," he sighed, shaking his head and staring at the court. "In addition to his play, I also notice that his memory isn't all that good when he comes late."

"Can you give me an example?" she asked.

"When I spoke with him on one of the mornings he slept in," Tom recalled, "it was like he forgot about our conversation from the previous day or week. At first, I thought it was because of some medicine he's taking…or not taking. I can't explain it but I do know that when he comes late to play with us he's not the same Mack. Now your friend, Flo Morgenstern, told me you like a good mystery. Do you think you could solve this one?"

Bess smiled at the thought that her reputation was something Flo bragged about.

"I do enjoy looking at the curious things people do," Bess nodded. "You're right about one thing, sleeping in on occasion is good for us. But it shouldn't change a person. Let me think about this dilemma and whether I can help you with this matter."

'None of us can figure it out," Mr. Gorman said with a shrug of his shoulders. "If you can find an answer for this…the fellas and I would be grateful to you. How can a guy play lights out pickleball one morning and then be the worst guy on the court the next? That's the mystery, Mrs. Bullock. Our next match is on Tuesday of next week. I think I speak for all the fellas when I say any help you can give would be appreciated."

"I'll see what I can learn between now and then," Bess promised.

She pondered the mystery that was presented to her as she walked back to the main building of the Honey Hills Center. When she arrived at the entrance to the main building, the air conditioning gave her a cool splash in the face. She roamed the hallways for a while, perspiration drying with each step. Once she felt refreshed, Bess made her way up to her apartment in the Tranquil Tower.

When the elevator reached the top floor, and the doors opened, she stepped over to a window that framed a perfect view of the Honey Hills grounds. She lingered by the window for a moment and thought about what Tom Gordon was asking of her. He was stumped over Mack's behavior, but didn't want to see Mack leave the group. There was a lot riding on Bess's help. In her mind, she could sense another person who was still counting on her help for a different matter. The face of Anita Mackley flashed for a second and with it, a swell of guilt over her diamonds not being found. It was the kind of unresolved mystery that nagged at Bess like a small bug too fast to swat.

"Oh, those diamonds!" Bess grumbled to herself.

While she wouldn't admit it to anyone, the fact that she had not found Anita's jewelry was beginning to weigh on her. On some level, it was causing her to question whether her advancing age was starting to affect her ability to solve mysteries. With her confidence on shaky ground, it would be a challenge to investigate a man that she didn't even know. Was she setting herself up for another unsolved case? Was she losing her knack for resolving little mysteries?

She decided not to dwell on such doubts. Instead, she kept her mind focused on learning more about the mysterious Mack McCall. Another meeting of her Bridge Club was scheduled to occur the following day. Perhaps, she thought, they could give her some insight about the pickleball player who had a knack for running late.

Chapter 11: ONE GOOD IDEA

With thoughts of two cases swirling in her head, Bess didn't sleep well that night. In fact, she rose at twilight and watched the sunrise from the windows in her bedroom. She quietly dressed, careful not to wake Chet, and began her day with a brisk walk around the grounds of the Honey Hills Center. Of course, no morning walk was complete without a stroll down Dogwood Lane. She wanted to check on her gardens and, if she worked up the courage, maybe sneak a peak in a window for a glimpse at the inside of her house.

When she turned the corner onto her street, she quickly spotted workers who appeared to be buzzing around Anita Mackley's home. While she always believed in the good in people, the mystery surrounding Anita and her missing jewels gave Bess reason to harbor a few suspicions about the workers.

Turning to her own home, Bess smiled and stepped into the front lawn. Morning dew nipping her ankles, she reached her front porch and paused. Fearing a mess inside, Bess took a deep breath before peering in through the window to her living room. She squinted into the glass where she saw drop cloths stretched across the floor. She also spotted some paint cans in the center of the room and a ladder propped against one wall. It appeared that her furniture was also covered by tarps. Bess was surprised at how calm she was at seeing so much clutter. While she expected some disarray, it was clearly not as bad as what she saw at Anita's house.

"A work in progress," Bess sighed to herself.

She stepped off the porch, walked to the backyard. The moment she saw her two gardens, an easy smile crept across her face.

"And a good morning to both of you," she quietly spoke to the plots.

She took small measured steps around each garden, carefully examining the details of what grew and what looked dry. Once she determined the state of her gardens, Bess pulled out a hose and turned on the water.

She stood in the burning sunlight, spraying her gardens while trying not to think about how hot the back of her neck was getting. After a few minutes of soaking both gardens, she took one last look at her home. An unspoken glance goodbye was good enough before heading back to the main building.

As she walked down Dogwood Lane, she thought about the disarray she saw in her house and wondered when she and Chet would be able to move back. She wiped some sweat from her brow as she followed the winding road that led her back to the main building. When she was close to the main building, the road took her by the pickleball court, which sat empty. Her mind began to turn away from the developments in her house to the questions Tom Gordon presented to her. Specifically, the questions about the curious Mack McCall. She then checked her watch and picked up her pace. It was almost time for her Bridge Club to begin.

Feeling like she was bathed in sweat, Bess thought about going back to her room and freshening up. The idea of a quick shower sounded appealing. However, as was often the case in the main building, her watch told her to head straight to her meeting.

"Another deadline to meet," Bess sighed to herself.

Soon she found herself walking into the Game Room where Rose Grumbine, Alma Crisp and Flo Morgenstern greeted her. Bess sat down at a round table listening to her friends chatter. At the center of the table she spotted a deck of cards waiting to be dealt. The second Bess sat down, Flo quickly scooped up the cards and began to shuffle.

"Did you just take a shower?" Flo asked.

"No," Bess replied, using the back of her hand to wipe away some beads of sweat from her cheek.

"You look...wet," Flo observed.

"Yes," Alma said, "and your face is red as a beet."

"Hot flash?" Rose grinned, pointing over to Bess.

"That's one of the worst cases of a hot flash I've ever seen," Alma chimed in. "I mean look at her...she's practically wet!"

"It's not a hot flash!" Bess quickly stated, fanning herself with her hand. "For heaven's sake, I'm not *that* young. I just got back from a walk. I wanted to check on my gardens this morning. I got an early start before the sun was up...and even though I left early the heat was still terrible. Thank the good Lord for air conditioning, ladies. The next time I take a morning walk, I'm going to have to get a much earlier start."

"You know," Alma began, "I was driving with Paul, my fiancé, to the store yesterday."

"We all know who Paul is," Flo observed. "Why do you have to say *fiancé* like that?"

"I just like to hear myself say the word, 'fiancé'" Alma giggled. "Anyway, there I was with Paul, my fiancé, driving one day and there was this woman riding her bike along Dogwood Lane. She cut across the street without seeing our car. Well, Paul was nice enough to stop and let her pass. Had it been someone younger talking on their phone, I bet they would have been too distracted to stop their car."

"Paul is always such a gentleman," Bess nodded.

"He is," Alma smiled. "But please be careful when you walk in the street, Bess. Some people aren't as nice as my fiancé."

Flo rolled her eyes after hearing the word *fiancé* again.

"I think it's madness for you to be out in this heat," Rose added and she gestured across the table to Bess. "I'm sorry but it really is too hot to do much of anything outside. I don't think it's good for you to be out there, Bess. Take that for what it's worth."

"Nice to know you're concerned," Bess smiled. "And next time, I'll be careful about walking in the street, Alma. I promise."

"Now that we're all here...can we start playing cards?" Flo asked before dealing the cards for the first round of the morning.

"That reminds me," Bess said, shifting in her seat to get a better look at Flo. "I understand we have a mutual friend. His name is Tom Gordon. He said he knows you. He also said you recommended me to help him resolve a curious problem. A matter that involves a member of his pickleball group?"

"Pickleball?" Flo asked, glancing up from her cards and squinting like she were in some kind of pain. "What's that?"

"It's like tennis, but with a smaller court and paddles," Bess explained.

"Do they eat pickles while they play?" Flo asked.

"I don't believe so," Bess answered.

"Do they bring pickles?" Rose asked, lowering her cards.

"There's no pickle...they just hit a ball," Bess stated.

"Then why do they call it...pickleball?" Rose asked.

"I...I don't know," Bess answered, putting the cards down.

"I don't like pickles!" Flo mumbled.

"Look," Bess said, rubbing her forehead, "forget about...pickles! The point is that Mr. Gordon enjoys playing this game with three other men in the mornings. Unfortunately, one of the men in the group has a bad habit of oversleeping. His name is Mack McCall. Now, according to Mr. Gordon, when Mack McCall arrives late he doesn't play very well. In fact, according to Mr. Gordon, Mack isn't just bad...he doesn't even remember the rules of pickleball. So, ladies, does anyone know this Mack McCall?"

There was silence around the table. Bess kept glancing from face to face, hoping to hear one word in reply to her query. After about a minute, she lowered her cards and could feel her face change expression in response to the silence.

"Ladies," Bess began, casting a look of disdain to her friends. "I thought we were the hub of social connections here at the Honey Hills community. We've been playing cards together for quite a few years. In all that time you've never let me down. You've always been able to talk to me about the residents who live here. Is today going to finally be the day that we don't know a resident? Are we slipping, ladies?"

"I wouldn't say we're *slipping*," Rose replied. "It's just the cycle of life here at the Honey Hills Center. There's a steady turnover rate of residents. I'd suppose it happens at any retirement home, Bess. Older residents die off and new ones move in. Mack McCall must be one of the newbies."

Bess sighed and laid down one card.

"When I first moved into this building years ago I had a pretty good idea of who everyone was around here," Bess stated. "When I didn't know a name I knew I could always ask one of you ladies...because you all seemed to know everyone. Now, to the best of my recollection, you'd always be quick to give me information on residents...until now."

Bess paused for a moment and looked around the table.

"Perhaps we need a younger member in our group to update us," Alma suggested.

"That might be," Bess said, "but at the moment I have to find a way to learn something about this...Mack McCall."

"Well, you know he plays pickleball," Flo shrugged while staring at her cards. "So there's one thing you know about him. Maybe you should approach him and ask for a lesson. Use some of that Bess Bullock charm and strike up a conversation with him. I bet he'd be more than happy to give you a lesson and answer some questions."

Bess sat back in her seat. She couldn't believe what she just heard. It was a brilliant idea. She laughed at the irony that such an insightful suggestion came from Flo's lips. The same Flo who was simply itching to play cards and wrap up the conversation.

"That's a very good idea, Flo," Bess grinned. "Perhaps *you* should take that lesson and get to the bottom of this mystery for me."

"No fun in that," Flo frowned, while she continued to stare at her cards. "I was a professional blackjack dealer at a casino, not a professional investigator. You do the detective work and...maybe we can all get back to playing some cards this morning."

"I will look into calling for a lesson...but I think I might need a partner to help me," Bess grinned and she turned to her right. "My arthritic knee has been flaring up so I won't be able to move very well. Who would like to help? How about you, Alma?"

Alma, who was always eager to listen to Bess's investigations, was all smiles upon hearing the invitation.

"You're asking *me* to help you with a case?" Alma asked.

"Yes," Bess nodded.

"Being retired means I don't have to check my calendar," Alma laughed. "Of course the answer is yes."

Chapter 12: FREEDOM

Later that evening, Bess called Tom Gordon and made the suggestion that he arrange for Alma to get a lesson from Mack McCall. Tom agreed on their plan and said he would schedule a lesson with Mack.

The very next morning, Bess and Alma found themselves seated in two red Adirondack chairs next to the pickleball courts. It was a surprisingly cool morning, which was a blessing since they had to wait for Mack to arrive.

"He's late," Bess said, checking her watch.

"Maybe he doesn't want to come outside," Alma suggested. "With the heat wave we've been having this summer, I don't think I'd like to be out here, either."

"That's a good theory," Bess said, "but someone who doesn't like the heat would be more motivated to arrive early. The fact he's coming late just means the sun will be up higher and the sunshine will be stronger. Since he's been playing pickleball all summer, I'd be willing to say the heat just doesn't bother him."

"So how would you like me to help you with this case?" Alma asked, rubbing her hands together in anticipation of her chance to help Bess with an investigation.

"As I said during Bridge Club, my knee has been bothering me," Bess explained. "I'd like you to take the lesson from Mack while I watch him and ask a few questions."

"I don't care for pickles," Alma said and her eyes squinted together. "I hope he doesn't ask me to eat one."

"For the last time, there *are* no pickles," Bess replied.

"Then maybe I'll ask him why they don't use a pickle," Alma smiled.

"You don't like pickles, Alma, so why even ask?" Bess observed.

"If I'm going to learn the game, Bess, I'd better know why the sport is called what it's called. You know me...I'm always curious," Alma defended.

"I guess that's why we get along so well," Bess sighed.

The moment they finished their quick exchange they saw Mack McCall step out from the main building. His round stomach, concealed beneath a tight-fitting red sports shirt, bounced as he strolled onto the court. Between the red shirt, and his round physique, Bess thought he looked like a walking tomato.

"Good morning, ladies!" he called out with a friendly tone and he followed up those words with a pleasant smile. "A friend of mine tells me you want a lesson on pickleball?"

"We do," Alma called back.

"My name is Mack McCall," he stated and his eyes fixed on Alma first before turning to Bess. She noticed how his eyes trailed down and stopped on her shoes and white slacks, then moved up to her short-sleeved blouse. "Tom Gordon says you two ladies are interested in learning the game. Lesson number one is that you have to wear the right clothes to play pickleball. Don't you have any shorts to wear? Some sneakers for running in? It's hot out here so you want to be comfortable to play."

"My friend is taking the lesson," Bess said, gesturing to Alma. "I'm only here to watch and learn."

"I see," Mack said, stepping over to Alma. He slowly nodded while looking at her sneakers, short skirt and a loose-fitting blouse. "What's your name?"

"Alma Blough," she stated.

"Well, Alma," he said, looking her up and down, "at least *you* look like you're dressed more appropriately than your friend. Do you have any questions before we begin?"

"How did they come up with the name for pickleball?" Alma quickly asked. "I'm not going to have to eat a pickle this morning, am I?"

"That's funny!" Mack laughed. "No, you won't be eating pickles. Now there are a few stories about where the name came from. The one I like is that the sport was named after a dog. They say the inventor of pickleball had a dog named Pickle. He must have really loved that dog since he incorporated the name into the sport."

"I like dogs more than pickles," Alma smiled and she took one step closer to Mack. "So...how do I play?"

"Yes," Bess nodded. "I was watching you play with your friends the other day and I couldn't figure out the rules."

"There are just a few rules to remember," Mack said before handing Alma a wooden paddle. "You're gonna need one of these for starters."

"I think my teacher had one of these in school," Alma laughed. "Of course, I was a well-behaved student. Always followed the rules so I never had to get paddled."

"Well, you won't be hitting anyone with this kind of a paddle," Mack explained without even cracking a smile. He gestured to the other side of the net at the green court with white lines on it. "In fact, you're going to use this paddle to hit a ball over the net. When you hit it, you'll want to keep the ball inside those lines on the court on the other side of the net."

With that comment, Mack picked up a ball from the court, walked to one side of the net, dropped the ball and hit it over the net. The wooden paddle made a loud "crack" when it hit the plastic ball. Bess watched the ball land in the middle of the court and roll to the fence behind the court.

For the next few minutes, Bess and Alma simply stood and listened to Mack go on about the game. He explained the scoring system. He demonstrated how to swing the paddle. He was very detailed in his instructions. Bess was impressed with everything he knew about the rules. He also showed good form when he swung. She was fascinated with all the different ways he showed Alma how to hit the ball. It was clear to Bess that Mack was quite knowledgeable about the game. In about a half-hour Mack had given a very thorough first lesson. The way Alma was hitting the ball, she appeared to be a natural.

With the temperature rising, and sweat building up on her face, Bess was relieved to see Mack finally check his watch and announce that the lesson was over. Alma thanked Mack more than once and appeared to really enjoy the instruction. Together the three of them headed for the main building. While they walked, Bess could hear Alma asking more questions to Mack. From what Bess could tell, Mack was patient and sounded very happy to answer everything Alma could think of.

Once inside the main building Bess and Alma continued to follow Mack through the hall. Bess made a mental note of every turn they made while they followed Mack back to his room. Eventually, the three of them turned a corner and Mack paused in front of a door that had the number 945. When he cracked open the door, Bess and Alma followed him inside his room.

"If you want another lesson just give me a call," Mack said, before handing out a slip of paper with his phone number on it.

"I'll remember that," Alma smiled, taking the paper.

"Thank you, Mister McCall," Bess nodded.

"It was a pleasure, ladies," Mack smiled. "Thank you for waiting around. I apologize for being late."

Mack McCall offered one last friendly smile before opening the door for them to exit his room.

"Bess," Alma whispered as they walked up the hallway. "You didn't even ask him one question. What kind of detective are you?"

"The kind who observes people," Bess quickly answered. "Sometimes I find answers without asking questions, Alma. This morning...I spotted quite a few things about Mr. McCall to resolve some of my questions. They're details I'll remember the next time I see him."

Chapter 13: A GOOD MORNING TO BE LATE

On the next morning that Mack McCall was scheduled to play pickleball with his friends, Bess decided to linger by the courts while on her morning walk. She was curious to see if this would be a morning when Mack would come on time or if he'd be running late.

As she approached the pickleball court she could see just three men standing on the court. A few steps closer, she recognized Tom Gordon as being one of the men. He was standing with two of his friends. She noticed how one of them had his arms folded. Another was leaning against the fence. Tom was chatting with both of them while he held his paddle in one hand and a ball in the other.

"Oh dear," Bess mumbled to herself.

She walked up to the fence where she noticed how one man kept checking his watch and turning to the doors that led into the main building. Tom Gordon glanced over and spotted Bess. The look on his face told her how he was feeling.

"If you're wondering why we're just standing around here yapping...it's because of Mack!" he called out.

Bess nodded in reply. She could sense the tension in his voice and the expression on the faces of the other players underscored the frustration.

"Should I go look for him?" Bess asked in a soft voice. "I know where his room is."

The very second she finished her statement, the door to the main building swung open and Mack McCall finally stepped outside. She smiled at him when he approached. She walked over to the gate leading onto the courts and opened it for him.

"You're late, Mack," Bess whispered.

He turned his head to Bess for a split second. There was no change of expression on Mack's face. In fact, he looked like he didn't value her words all that much. He stepped by her with a scowl. The second his foot touched the court a broad smile quickly graced his face. He walked up to each player apologizing profusely for his tardiness.

"Sorry for holding you up, fellas," he explained, taking a few practice swings to loosen up his arm. "I got a phone call from my grandson that I couldn't avoid. Once that boy starts talking he just doesn't stop."

"That's fine," Tom mumbled.

"We've heard that excuse before," one of the men grumbled.

"Tell that grandson to call you back," the other man suggested.

"He's only five!" Mack laughed, waving one hand up to the sky. "He gets up with the sun and he likes to talk to his grandpa, I guess."

It was clear to Bess that this was an awkward moment. Mack was trying hard to make light of the moment, but the other men on the court were hot and in no mood for jokes.

"You ready to show Bess how good you can play?" Tom asked.

"Who?" Mack replied.

"You know…Bess," Tom repeated and he gestured out the fence to where she was standing. "You gave her and her friend a lesson yesterday."

"Oh….yeah…Bess," Mack said with barely a glance in her direction.

As play began, Bess sat down and became engrossed in the pickleball match. She watched the frustration melt away from the players once they started playing points. As the game commenced, she found the laughter of everyone involved to be quite entertaining. Eventually her attention turned to Mack.

With each point, she watched how Mack played and how he moved. After a number of points went by, her mind began drawing some conclusions. Her first conclusion was that he wasn't playing as well as the other players. After watching more points come and go, she attributed his poor play to his slow footwork. He was clearly having trouble getting to the ball. He wasn't on his toes so his movement wasn't as fluid as yesterday, she thought. Footwork was the kind of detail that only a Waltzing Club member like herself would notice.

In between points, Bess also watched how the players interacted with each other. She noticed how they continued to chat, joke and call out to one another, how they made jokes and referenced conversations from previous days. Mack was a bit more standoffish. While he listened, he remained quiet and reserved and didn't offer any meaningful words to any of the other men. He wasn't as chatty as he had been for Alma's lesson.

Another clue came in the way he swung at the ball. His form appeared to be less controlled than it was during his lesson with Alma. In fact, Bess thought, he looked like he was trying to swat a bug when he swung at the ball. It wasn't the smooth easy motion she saw the previous day. Perhaps, Bess concluded, that was why most of his hits were off center. In her opinion, there was something about Mack McCall that just didn't match the details she observed yesterday.

As the morning hours went by, the heat from the sun grew stronger. Fearing a sunburn on the back of her neck, Bess decided to duck inside to the air conditioning to cool herself off. Once inside she realized it was nearly impossible to see out to the courts or to hear the conversations being exchanged. Feeling a few beads of sweat forming on her forehead, Bess knew she would need more time away from the sun.

"I should get a drink," she mumbled.

With the thought of a cool drink of water enticing her, Bess began to walk down the hallway in search of a water fountain or a nurses' station. The irony was not lost on Bess that for the first time since coming back to the main building, there were no nurses in sight. A few years earlier, when she lived in the same building, there were nurses everywhere. Perhaps, she reasoned, it was due to the smaller number of residents.

Continuing her quest down the hall, Bess noticed that the doors on either side of the hall were numbered in the nine hundreds.

"This is Mack's wing," Bess whispered to herself.

While staring at the door, she felt her curiosity quickly quench her thirst. Following the numbers on each door, she turned down an adjoining hallway noting how the numbers were getting larger. A few people passed by but her eyes remained fixed on the doors. Soon she arrived at the number 945.

"Here it is," Bess whispered to herself.

She paused in front of the closed door, knowing that behind it was Mack McCall's room. She stood at the door, debating about whether to sneak inside to look for more details about her mysterious pickleball player.

"He'll never know," she told herself.

As she grabbed hold of the door knob, her eyes were drawn to something curious on the floor. The light slipping out from under the bottom of the door began to flicker. She remained perfectly still and saw the flickering stop then start again. She placed her ear on the door and heard something that caused her grip on the door knob to tighter.

"Was that a man's cough?" Bess whispered to herself.

She slowly turned the door knob and pushed open the door. She stepped in the doorway and, in less than a second, stood in awe of what she had just found.

"What are you doing here?" she asked.

At first, she thought she was delusional from the heat. After a few seconds, she realized what she was seeing wasn't a hallucination. Sitting in a chair in the middle of the room was the man she had just left outside playing pickleball. The man who was always running late. Staring at her entering the room was Mack McCall.

Chapter 14: A PICKLE FOR A THOUGHT

Mack's eyes locked on her. The expression on his face was not all that warm or welcoming. In fact, he didn't even look surprised when she entered the room. Yet despite his cold expression, Bess could feel herself being drawn in from the hallway.

Her eyes started picking up on details. Mack didn't look like he just stepped into his room. In fact, he looked very relaxed, wearing entirely different clothes. Her curiosity over his appearance was overriding her good manners, leading her to continue entering the room without his permission. Like a bee to honey, she simply couldn't resist.

She moved to the chair where Mack was seated, but he didn't say a word. Her eyes darted around his frame, lingering on the khaki pants and blue sport shirt he wore. His face didn't look sweated from playing pickleball. In fact, he looked very calm and cool. The only expression she could gather from his face was one of a small child who just got caught with his hand in the cookie jar.

"Mack?" Bess asked, stepping closer. "What are you doing here?"

He remained silent.

"I mean...*how* can you be here?" Bess asked, her head tilting to one side as she stepped in front of him. "You're supposed to be outside with Tom Gordon playing pickleball with your friends. In fact, I just saw you out there when I came in for a drink. You don't look sweated. And...how did you change your clothes so quickly? Something isn't right about this. You looked confused. Do you remember me?"

"You're...Mrs. Bullock...right?" he asked and his eyes went up and down when he said her name.

She nodded.

He smiled and pointed to her dress.

"I see you're still not dressed for pickleball," he observed. "That was the only tip I gave you from that lesson...and you still aren't following my advice."

"So you do remember me," Bess said and she pointed out the window. "A few hours ago you acted like you didn't know me when I spoke to you at the court. You walked right by and barely acknowledged me."

Mack had no reply to her statement. His silence told her something. She stepped closer to him and watched his eyes flick across the room to a small table under a window. She walked over to the table where a collection of framed photographs sat.

Some were set in wooden frames while others were in clear plastic ones. Most of the pictures were contemporary, filled with colorful shots of what she guessed were Mack's children and grandchildren. Smiling happy faces filled her vision. However, one photo looked different from the rest.

It was the only black and white picture on the table. She leaned closer and noticed it was of two young boys, dressed in white-t-shirts and jeans, with arms wrapped around each other. Bess stepped closer to the picture, picked it up and studied the image for a moment. She examined the smiling faces of the boys then turned and looked back at Mack.

"I think these two boys look an awful lot alike," Bess commented, pointing at the picture. "They appear to have the same height, same hair color, even the same smile."

"Yes," Mack replied.

"Is that you?" Bess asked.

Mack remained silent.

"And the other boy?" she asked

"My brother," Mack replied.

Bess put the picture back on the table and turned to Mack.

"Your brother?" Bess asked and she pointed to the door of his room. "So you have a twin? I'm guessing the man I saw playing pickleball outside with Tom Gordon and your friends is the same twin brother. Isn't he? Or maybe we should walk outside and ask."

Mack again looked away from Bess and didn't answer. His eyes dropped to his hand and he jingled a set of car keys he was holding. He stood up and took one step towards the door. Bess quickly stepped in front of Mack.

"Tell me the truth or I'll invite them into your room," Bess warned.

"I don't have a lot of time to talk about this," Mack stated, twirling the keys on his one finger. "Can we meet back here tomorrow? I'll have more time to answer your questions tomorrow."

"Wait!" Bess snapped and she walked over to the doorway. She stood in the doorway, blocking him from leaving. "Before you go anywhere I have a few questions I'd like you to answer. You say you're short on time? Then answer my questions quickly."

"I'm sorry but I don't have time for this," Mack said and he tried to step around her but Bess stood her ground in the doorway.

"You're lying to your friends!" Bess said in a very direct tone. "Tom Gordon told me you all are close…like brothers. I guess you forgot to mention you had an identical twin to them. For that reason alone, you should explain yourself. Or would you rather walk outside with me and share this news with your friends? I suspect this isn't the first time you've had your brother come here and play pickleball for you. I just want to know why he's doing it. I've seen both of you play and you're clearly the better player."

Mack stepped back from the doorway and took a deep breath.

"I have my reasons," he quietly stated, checking his wrist watch.

"Then tell me if you want to leave," Bess said, extending her arms and gripping the doorframe with both hands.

"Can we talk while we walk?" Mack asked, pointing over her shoulder towards the hallway. "I really *must* go somewhere. It's...a health issue. Could you walk with me while I talk and I'll answer your questions."

"Fine," Bess answered, stepping aside and following him out of the room. "So let's start with the obvious, why is your brother playing pickleball for you?"

"It's a long and painful story," he sighed while walking beside her.

"I'm listening," Bess said, walking faster to keep up.

"When I first began playing pickleball with the fellas, it was a lot of fun," Mack explained. "We really hit it off. When we weren't playing we were doing things off the court, too. Stopping in each other's rooms to chat. Watching sports on TV together. Talking about our thoughts on our last pickleball match. Then one morning, I started to get some elbow pain after playing. That week I tried taking an anti-inflammatory medicine but it didn't help. I kept taking medicine so when it was time to play, I was ready to give it a whirl. I played hurt and it got worse the next morning."

He paused for a moment but continued walking down another long hallway.

"So why didn't you tell them?" Bess asked.

"Those guys are like brothers to me and I didn't want to let them down," he stated. "I know they look forward to playing as much as I do. That's why I put in a call to my brother to fill in for me. I gave him a few lessons and taught him the rules. The first time he played for me, I was able to take some extra time to rest my arm…and my elbow did feel better the following week. I played with no pain that day. Then the following week the pain came back. So, that's what my brother and I came to an agreement. If I have a day when my elbow pain flares up, I take some aspirin and call my brother and take the week off. It's not that far for him to drive and he likes the exercise."

"So he doesn't live in the Honey Hills community?" Bess asked.

"No," Mack replied. "He lives in Franklin with his wife."

"Well, that's an hour away. That would explain why he sometimes runs late," she nodded. "I still don't know why you're so secretive about this…arrangement? Why not tell your friends that your brother is going to play for you when your elbow hurts? Why not say, 'he's my brother but he's not very good.'"

"To be honest, I was worried about them replacing me with another player," Mack smiled. "The first time it happened a doctor told me to take a month off. A whole month! That's too long for me to stay away from my gang. They'd replace me if I didn't keep playing. I'm grateful my brother is able to help me out. This elbow thing should clear itself up by next week. Then I'll be able to play like normal and no one will be the wiser."

"Until you hurt it again," Bess pointed out. "We're not getting any younger, Mack. Our bodies don't heal the way they used to. Besides, your friends have already noticed that your brother isn't as good a player as you. Not as personable either. Because he's such a poor player some of them want to replace you and move on with another player."

"Replace me?" Mack asked, an expression of surprise coming over his face.

"I'm afraid so," Bess replied.

"Well, I can give my brother more lessons," Mack quickly suggested. "He's a good athlete. He can improve."

"What about telling the truth?" Bess suggested.

"I can't tell them the truth," Mack stated.

"Why?" Bess asked.

"I'm about to show you," Mack replied and pointed ahead of them.

Bess realized they were approaching the main entrance. Mack opened the door and quickly stepped out into the heat of the day, Bess following behind him. He led her into the parking lot and she watched him linger beside a bright red convertible. He slipped on some sunglasses, hopped in the driver's seat and pulled out the keys.

"What are you doing?" she asked.

"This is my brother's car," Mack explained. "The mornings he comes to play for me I get to borrow his car and go for a drive."

"Does he know?" Bess asked.

"Of course he knows," Mack laughed, slipping on some sunglasses. "I can't tell any of the nurses what I'm doing or they'll stop me from leaving. You ever notice how we residents are always considered too old and confused to know how to have fun. Have you ever noticed that?"

"All the time," Bess replied with a grin.

"When my brother comes, I get to walk out those front doors, drive my brother's sports car and spend the morning being a normal person around town.

Sometimes I even go through a drive thru and eat a burger. When's the last time you had a good greasy burger and fries with too much salt? You can't get that kind of food around here."

"I thought you said you had a medical appointment?" Bess asked.

"I do," Mack grinned. "This is my mental health day."

"I won't argue with that," Bess laughed.

"I like the occasional chance to escape for a morning of freedom," he continued, tapping the steering wheel with his hand. "You see, my children pushed me into this place because they wanted peace of mind. At my age, I'm perfectly fine mentally and physically. So why shouldn't I be allowed to escape every once in a while?"

"Why indeed?" Bess laughed.

He looked at her and the smile left his face.

"Is my secret safe with you?" he asked.

"Which one?" Bess asked. "The fact that your arm hurts every other week or that you enjoy your freedom so much you'll continue to lie about your brother? As I said, Mack, which lie would you like me to keep for you?"

Mack McCall stared at her and again grew silent. He took out a key and slipped it into the ignition. He put on some sunglasses and smiled.

"Both please," he grinned.

Bess shook her head at his comment and his lack of honesty.

"Would you like to go out for a burger, Bess?" Mack asked. "I can turn on the radio and we can drive with the wind in our hair."

"Another time," she smiled, waving at him. "Now go enjoy your freedom before your brother finishes playing. And remember…promise me you'll give him some lessons. You don't want him to play so badly that the other fellas boot you out of the group."

"I promise," he replied.

Suddenly, Mack turned the key in the ignition and gunned the engine. It sounded like a bear growling. He gave her one last wave before speeding away, car shimmering in the sunlight.

Bess simply stood and grinned at the sight of a fellow resident escaping the confines of the main building for a burger and a dose of freedom. She thought about his need to go beyond these walls. She thought about the last time she and Chet went into town for groceries or a bite to eat. She heard Mack's car accelerate up the street and one word popped into her head and out her lips.

"Freedom."

Chapter 15: MYSTERY BY THE FIELD

Bess thought about Mack McCall's lack of honesty for the rest of the day. While she disagreed with his lies, she could clearly understand his desire for freedom once a week. The image of Mack driving away with a big smile on his face, enjoying his freedom in a fancy sports car tickled her heart. It even inspired her to ask Chet if they could get their own car from their home on Dogwood Lane and take it out for a spin. She brought it up in bed one night, suggesting they drive into town the next morning for breakfast. It was the kind of idea that put smiles on both of their faces as they drifted off to sleep.

Unfortunately, the morning did not cooperate. Bess woke to the gentle sound of rain tapping on the window by her bed. Rather than walking through the rain to get their car, Bess and Chet resigned themselves to the reality of having another breakfast in the Dining Hall. The clock on her nightstand provided enough motivation to get out of bed. She slipped out from under the sheets, well aware of how much time they had until breakfast. Looking out the window at the steady rain, Bess felt like a child wishing the weather would improve so she and Chet could get their car. She stood by the window scanning the sky, waiting for some patch of blue to appear through all the gray clouds. It wasn't a heavy rain, but simply the kind of steady light drops that farmers like to keep their fields moist.

When she walked out to the living room, she was surprised to find her husband already up and dressed. Wearing khakis and a short sleeved blue shirt, Chet was settled into the couch watching the business news on TV. He appeared to be the picture of contentment. He looked up at her and flipped off the TV. He put his hand up to his ear and smiled.

"Do you hear that?" he asked, gesturing to the window.

"No," Bess replied.

He got up, took her hand and led her to a window next to his couch. He stepped beside her and pointed to a cardinal perched on a tree branch not far from their window. Chet cracked open the window and the bird's sweet call filled the room with melodic tones.

"How beautiful," Bess sighed, staring at the red bird.

"Yes, it is," Chet smiled. "He's been right outside the window singing for a while."

It was a moment to savor for both of them. Perhaps the best moment they'd experienced since moving to the main building. After about a minute, the cardinal finally leaned forward and dove from the branch where a gentle breeze carried it away. Bess smiled at the sight. Chet tipped his wrist and tapped one finger on his watch.

"We'd better get down there for breakfast," he sighed, closing the window.

"Already?" she asked, the smile from watching the bird melting off her face. "Oh, Chet, how I'd like to skip the Dining Hall and just…snack on something."

"We don't have a kitchen," Chet complained. "If it were possible, I'd be happy with spreading some peanut butter on a bagel, or scrambling up some eggs. The only downside of this lovely apartment is that there's no working kitchen to use, just a small fridge."

"I'm sure that's how they motivate us to go back to the Dining Hall," Bess chuckled. "Starving us will always make bland food taste better."

"You might be right," Chet replied. "If they don't build kitchens in the rooms, and they don't provide some fruits or snacks, then we're more likely to be starving when we go to the Dining Hall. I wonder if the chef came up with that strategy to compensate for his or her less than adequate culinary skills?"

"Oh, Chet," Bess scolded, "I'm sure whoever they are, they're doing their best."

"Whoever it is…they aren't as talented as you in the kitchen," Chet smiled.

"You're sweet," Bess said and she glanced at herself in a mirror and frowned at what was looking back at her. "Well, if you're that hungry, Chet, go down and find a table for us. I want to put some makeup on before I leave. Afraid I slept a bit too late this morning. I need to make myself presentable."

Chet kissed her on the cheek before slipping out the door for the elevator.

Bess took a deep breath, looked in the mirror and noted that it was the first time since moving to the Tranquil Tower that she was alone in the apartment. She drew in her breath, savored the silence, and combed her hair. When finished, she put on some lipstick then headed to the window by her bed and frowned at the dark sky.

"A day fit for sweet singing birds…but not much else," she sighed.

The gray clouds appeared to be seamless, reminding her of a lumpy wool blanket that had been stretched over the countryside. The clouds cast a steady light rain, which made her grateful that her gardens were enjoying some much-needed nourishment. She was also happy that the Tranquil Tower was part of the main building, so she wouldn't have to venture out for anything. She checked her watch and knew she had to meet up with Chet in the Dining Hall.

She walked out to the elevator, pressed a button and waited for it to arrive. Living on the top floor of the Tranquil Tower required a good deal of patience whenever they needed the elevator. Three times a day, she and Chet had to occupy their mind with other thoughts while waiting for it to arrive. Sometimes when she waited, Bess would look out a window next to the elevator.

With the elevator still in transit, Bess stepped up to the window and looked out on the mountain ridge beyond the farm fields. She noticed the way the mist lingered over the ridge like a sheer veil. She also looked down at the full green farm fields soaking up the rain. Then she saw something that caused her to draw in her breath and step closer to the window.

"Who is that?" Bess whispered.

Standing at the edge of the field, she spied a woman holding an umbrella. The woman stood perfectly still, right next to the field. She wore a red jacket, but what caught Bess's eye was the tint of blue-gray hair that Bess had seen a week earlier. It appeared to be the same woman she saw standing in the same spot on a sweltering hot today.

"Why is she back again?" Bess asked herself.

She took a long lingering gaze at the woman standing by the field. Regardless of rain or a heat wave, it was clear that this woman was determined to not let the elements bother her. Once again she was enduring bad weather to stand and stare at a field. It was tempting for Bess to grab her umbrella, duck outside and confront the woman to find out what was at the root of this odd behavior. Bess was extremely curious to know why this woman was being drawn back to the same location.

A bell sounded and Bess noticed the elevator doors were opening. She checked her watch then stepped inside the elevator and pressed a button for the ground floor. A moment later the doors opened and she walked out. She could smell the aroma of breakfast dripping from the air. She hesitated by the entrance to the Dining Hall, contemplating whether or not to meet Chet or step outside to speak with the woman.

"Never enough time," Bess sighed, glancing at her watch again.

She could see Chet sitting at a table by himself. In that moment, her heart won out over her instincts. She entered the Dining Hall to join her husband and wait for breakfast to be served.

Chapter 16: A PLEASANT BREAKFAST

She could tell by the expression on her husband's face that they were in agreement over what filled their mouths. For the first time since they were moved to the Honey Hills Center's main building, Bess and Chet were actually enjoying a meal that appeared to satisfy both of their pallets.

It was a breakfast casserole, made with sausage, eggs, cheese and a sauce that was mildly spicy. In addition to the casserole, there was also a warm biscuit that melted in their mouths. From the first bite, Bess could tell it was finally going to be a meal she would enjoy. While it was a big meal for breakfast, Bess was happy with the quality of the food.

"What do you think?" Bess grinned, leaning across the table.

"I...I don't know what to say," Chet said, dabbing his chin with a napkin. "I can't believe I'm going to say these words...but I'm actually enjoying this meal."

"Me too," Bess laughed.

"Well," Chet replied, "After a few weeks, I guess someone in the kitchen was bound to hit one meal out of the ballpark. I just can't figure out why it would be breakfast?"

"Perhaps the chef is a morning person," Bess laughed, and she tapped the edge of her plate with one finger. "This food tasted...inspired to me."

"It isn't as bland as the other meals we've had," Chet nodded and he checked his watch before standing up from the table. "I have to meet with some people about our plans for the next Waltzing Club meeting. I assume you don't want to join me?"

"You assume correctly," Bess replied before taking another sip of coffee. "I like to dance...but a Waltzing Club meeting that involves filling out papers just doesn't sound as interesting. I'm going back to our room and gather some laundry together, Chet. Do you know we haven't had the staff wash any of our clothes since we moved here?"

"You always keep tabs on the important things," Chet said before stepping next to her and kissing her. "I'll see you after my meeting."

Bess leaned back in her seat and watched Chet leave the Dining Hall. She held a mug of coffee in both hands and took a moment to soak in her surroundings. To her left, there were four ladies sitting around one table not speaking to one another while they ate. They also appeared to be enjoying the meal, perhaps even more than each other's company. In a back corner, she spied a husband and wife who were seated at a small table. They were huddled close to each other speaking about something. Noticing their hand gestures, Bess could only guess that the discussion was important. Near the center of the room, she spotted one man sitting at a table by himself, smiling at something outside a window. It was quite fascinating for Bess, who always enjoyed observing the curious nature of people.

Elbows planted on the table, she took a long sip of coffee when a body entered her line of vision. She looked up just as the person was sitting down in Chet's vacant seat. When Bess managed to focus on the person's face, she quickly recognized who was seated across from her. She took one big gulp of the coffee in her mouth and tried to collect her thoughts and remain calm.

"Anita?" Bess said, a little surprised.

"Have you found my diamonds yet?" Anita asked, glancing around to see if anyone had overheard her question.

Bess could feel her face grow hot and her heart began to beat a little faster.

"No," Bess replied before sipping the last of her coffee. "Where's Cliff?"

"Playing poker with some friends," Anita stated while pushing Chet's empty plate to the center of the table. "It's been over a week since I talked to you, Bess."

"Really?" Bess smiled in an attempt to lighten the mood. "You know how it is when you're retired, Anita…time flies."

"Have you forgotten about my problem?" Anita asked. She leaned across the table, her dark eyes locking on Bess without blinking once. "I must have those diamonds back. Those workers will be done with our homes in a few weeks and then they'll be gone. You must press them to find the culprit. From what everyone says about you…I thought you would have moved a little faster on my case."

"You gave me quite a list of suspects," Bess replied, an image of the workers scattered around Dogwood Lane flashing in her head. "Things like this take time. I don't solve mysteries with magic. There's a process involved."

"It seems to me you're not even giving it your full attention," she replied.

"Why would you say that?" Bess asked.

"Because you should be asking more questions!" Anita said, her voice growing slightly sharper. "When I take my morning walks, I don't see you anywhere in the neighborhood. I think you should be out there every morning spying on workers and telling me which ones you suspect. At the very least, you should be giving me more reports about what you're doing...but you're not."

"Sometimes, Anita, things come at their own pace," Bess fibbed while she struggled to hide any appearance of doubt in resolving the case.

"Well, it's just not what I expected from you," Anita fumed.

"Let me tell you something," Bess replied, carefully placing her coffee mug back on its saucer. "I work at my own pace. It's a pace I find sufficient. If you're not happy with it, you're more than welcome to pursue other avenues. However, it seems to me that you don't have many options. You can either trust me, go to the police *or* speak with the Honey Hills security department. Since you prefer not to involve the police or security, that leaves you with me. Because of the wide range of suspects, it's going to take a good deal of time to shrink my list of suspects. While I may be involved in other matters, I promise you my thoughts are still engaged with your case."

Anita glanced down at her hand and nervously tapped her fingers on the table before abruptly getting up and leaving. Bess had a suspicion as to what happened to the diamonds but did not want to share her theory with Anita. There were a few details she had to attend to first before revealing her suspicions.

Chapter 17:   CURIOUS FOR CLUES

The next morning Bess was feeling curious. She kept thinking about her exchange with Anita. Deep down inside, she knew Anita was right on one count. It had been a long time since Bess walked back to her neighborhood. A stretch of rainy weather made it impossible for her get to Dogwood Lane. However, the weather was changing for the better, which presented her with an opportunity.

Waking up early, Bess was happy to finally see blue sky filling the windows to her bedroom. The nice weather gave a nudge to her inquisitive nature. She began to think about her home and all the days that passed since she saw it. What changed? What remained the same? Her instincts were curious about the possibilities. She stepped up to the window, looked out on the Honey Hills grounds, and decided it was a good day to take stock of her home and silence her curiosity.

With Chet at his meeting, Bess returned to her room, slipped on her walking shoes and headed back downstairs. The moment she stepped outside the main building, she was greeted by a blazing sun. The heat didn't dampen her spirts, though. She was excited to start her morning walk, knowing exactly what her destination was going to be.

Eventually, she came across a sign for Dogwood Lane at a corner. She turned off Magnolia Lane and felt her lips curl into a smile, sensing her proximity. When she reached her house, Bess was careful to peek through a few windows to see if any workers were inside. After looking in two windows, she simply grew tired of acting like a cat burglar sneaking around her own home. It was her house and she had a right to see what was inside.

"A quick peek won't hurt anyone," Bess mumbled to herself, slipping her house key into the front door and opening it.

As soon as the door opened, she stepped inside and quickly closed it. Silence was the first thing she noticed. It seemed like her house was giving her the "silent treatment" for being away so long. Bess stood and took in her surroundings. In front of her, a few gray cloth tarps were draped over her furniture. Her eyes were also drawn to some wires dangling from the ceiling just above her dining room table. It appeared that the old chandelier was gone, which prompted her to shake her head.

"I loved that light fixture," she complained to herself.

She took a deep breath and tried to soak in more details. The slight smell of paint. The new drapes that hung over one window. Her couch, which had been moved to a different wall. In one sense, it felt good to be home. However, it was hard to take in all the changes that were being made.

"Why couldn't they ask me first?" Bess sighed.

Out of the corner of her eye, a figure appeared from the shadows. Bess turned and was shocked to find an older man walking out from the far end of the hallway. She jumped and covered her mouth at this unexpected guest.

Stepping into the light, the man's face was red, glowing with sweat. His short white hair glistened with perspiration. He was taller than Bess, with thick arms that poked out from under a tight-fitting t-shirt. He was also holding a hammer. Suddenly, a younger woman stepped up beside the man. She was maybe in her mid-twenties and had a tattoo on her left forearm.

Upon seeing both unexpected workers, Bess stepped back instinctively and thought about heading for the front door. Her eyes grew wide and she fought her emotions to remain calm. She quickly made the distinction of knowing these weren't unwelcomed intruders. They were there doing a job. The man glared at Bess in a way that told her he was not happy with her appearance. Bess stood her ground.

"Hello," she quietly said with the sweetest smiles she could muster. "You two…are in my house."

The man's face got redder and he pointed at her with a thick crooked finger.

"You shouldn't be here!" he snapped.

The young woman standing next to him remained silent. She was shorter than the man and rail thin. Under her blond bangs were a pair of warm eyes looking at Bess. The young girl offered a smile and placed her hand on the older man's shoulder.

"Uncle Ben," the younger woman said, stepping between him and Bess. "I'm sure she's just curious about what's happening to her house. That's all."

"She knows she's not supposed to be here!" he advised, still speaking with a voice that bordered on anger. "We told the Honey Hills staff that residents must be removed from their homes and out of our way. We even had our lawyer draw up a letter stating as much. If one of them gets injured, then we get a phone call from a lawyer. That's why *she* shouldn't be here!"

The expression on his face, combined with his words and tone of voice, created a feeling of uneasiness that Bess hadn't experienced in a while. There was real tension in this moment, not the kind of silly tension brought on by arriving late in the Dining Hall. This man's eyes were locked on Bess and she was beginning to feel uncomfortable.

"I...I'm sorry," Bess quietly offered.

The man simply remained silent and continued to stare at her.

"Let me walk her out," the young woman said, gesturing for Bess to exit by way of the front door.

Bess quietly obliged, following the young woman out. They stood on the front porch together, Bess taking a deep breath before pointing back at her front door.

"He sounds like an angry fellow," Bess finally stated.

"That's my Uncle Ben," the woman smiled, nervously brushing her hand over her short blond hair. "For as long as I can remember, Uncle Ben has always been kind of high strung about stuff. He says he's passionate...but I think it's just his blood pressure. My name is Elizabeth, by the way."

"Nice to meet you," Bess smiled, folding her arms across her chest. "So you work with your uncle? That's a bit unusual to have relatives working for the same business."

"Not really," Elizabeth shrugged. "I'm related to a lot of people where I work. I have three of my uncles, four of my aunts, a lot of cousins and my dad all working with me on the houses along this street."

Bess could feel her eyebrows push together after hearing this fact.

"How is that possible?" she asked.

"Our construction company is a family business," Elizabeth shrugged. "My Dad and his brothers built this company. Over the years they hired a lot of the family to work for them. Coming to work, for me, it's like having a family reunion every week."

"I saw one gentleman who looked Amish," Bess spoke up. "Is he related to you?"

"Yes," she nodded. "That's my Uncle Jim. He actually married an Amish woman and decided to convert."

"I didn't know you could convert to the Amish faith," Bess said.

"It's very rare, but he did," Elizabeth explained.

"So everyone who works on this crew….is related to each other?" Bess asked.

"Pretty much," she nodded. "It was my Uncle Clayton's idea. You see, we're a close-knit family. Uncle Clayton figured if he hired only family, or people who married into the family, we'd work extra hard so we could all succeed together."

"That way your family relies on each other for their jobs," Bess nodded. "I'd suppose if one person chose not to put in a good day of work, or made lots of mistakes, or even stole something, it would affect the rest of the family."

"Believe me," Elizabeth grinned, "if one of my cousins did something stupid like stealing…the rest of us would know about it in a heartbeat. We're a big family but nothing is a secret between us. We're always in each other's business. Besides, my dad pays us well. We all have enough money. As far as I am concerned, nobody in our family needs to steal."

"So no one in your family is living paycheck to paycheck?" Bess asked.

"Harden Industries is the largest construction company in three counties," she explained. "My dad is Jack Harden. He pays all of us well. He's always picking up contracts for us. Everyone around here knows my dad so they call him all the time about construction bids and contracts. He's the first name up…or so my uncle says."

Bess nodded but could feel the heat begin to take hold. She glanced up at the blazing sun and squinted.

"And what's your name again?" she asked.

"Elizabeth Harden," she replied.

"It was a pleasure to meet you, Elizabeth," Bess said.

"You want me to walk you through your house?" Elizabeth asked. "I can show you what we've been working on this morning. Don't let Uncle Ben scare you off. I know he's loud...but he won't bite."

"I'd better get back to my apartment," Bess sighed, glancing up to the sky. "It feels like it's getting warmer by the minute, doesn't it? I should get back to the main building before I really start to sweat. I'm afraid air conditioning has become my best friend this summer, Elizabeth."

"Suit yourself," Elizabeth said before stepping back into Bess's house.

Bess stepped off the porch and headed down Dogwood Lane. While she walked, Bess thought about the claims she had just heard. Would one member of such a close-knit family really have the guts to steal diamonds from Anita? Were her relatives as rich as she thought? Were they really as meddlesome as she made them sound?

By the time she reached the main building, Bess had reviewed all of the observations and conversations she'd had with various workers over the week. She recalled every detail since leaving Dogwood Lane. Based on the facts as she saw them, Bess decided to rule out the workers. There simply weren't enough facts to suspect one of them of being the culprit. Instead, another candidate was taking shape in her mind.

Chapter 18: THE DARK DISCOVERY

The next morning was just as sunny as the last. In her heart, Bess had already known it was going to be a good morning regardless of the weather. She knew it because she was going to start the day by dancing with her husband.

Bess's favorite morning of the week began with a meeting of the Honey Hills Waltzing Club. The Waltzing Club would always hold a special place in her heart. It was the first club she joined after moving to the Honey Hills Retirement Center. It was also where she met and fell in love with her beloved Chet.

She first got to know him as the new president of the Waltzing Club. Among his many duties was to choose the music for each class, pick the dances for members to learn and select members to help him demonstrate the dances. At one meeting, he picked Bess out of a crowd of residents to help him demonstrate one particularly challenging waltz. They moved so smoothly together she felt like her toes were floating on air. From that first dance, she knew they were destined to remain partners on and off the dance floor.

Chet ran the Waltzing Club for four years, picking the dances they would try and the music they would listen to. One day, while still living on Dogwood Lane, Chet confided to Bess for the first time that he thought it would be best to relinquish his role as president. While he thoroughly enjoyed the position, he decided it was time to have someone new take over. Someone who could re-energize the Waltzing Club.

Eventually, Chet settled on a suitable replacement. He suggested a new resident, Mike "Mutt" Murphy, who was quite good at dancing at the meetings. Chet thought he'd make a fine president. In addition to being a proficient dancer, Mutt was always smiling, laughing, and chatting it up with other residents during the meetings. He was enthusiastic and always had ideas for moves to try and steps to add to a lesson. In short, he had all the creativity and energy that Chet was looking for in a new president.

The following week, after a meeting of the Waltzing Club, Chet told Bess he was going to speak with Mutt to gauge his interest in taking over as president. While he huddled with Mutt in a corner, Bess lingered at the other end of the large multipurpose room where they held their meetings. She stood there in the room, smiling and chatting with every member of the Waltzing Club. Once all the members were gone, she turned her attention to Chet.

At first glance, she watched Chet and Mutt's smiles move from stoic to genuine. She could sense the length of the conversation growing and she observed mutual good feelings. The jovial expressions and head nods told her an agreement had been made. She watched them fold their arms, sit down in a couple of chairs and settle into a dialogue that she could only guess would last for more than a few minutes.

Sensing that she had an abundance of time on her hands, Bess stepped out of the room, nodded to one friendly face in the hallway before finding a nearby sitting area. She exchanged pleasantries with some faces seated in couches and chairs. She took a few steps around the sitting area and began to take in her surroundings.

Located in one corner, she found a man playing a piano, filling the air with a lovely melody. Across the way, two ladies sat in separate chairs, staring at nothing in particular. Bess stepped over to a nearby window and glanced out at the farm fields and the sunshine.

"Another beautiful...hot day," she sighed to herself.

She wandered back to the doorway leading into the multipurpose room, where she saw Chet still talking with Mutt about the Waltzing Club. Both men seemed deep in thought. Bess wrapped her arms around her chest and took a deep breath.

"This could take a while," she sighed.

She checked her watch before turning back to the sitting area one more time. When she heard the piano player begin to perform *My Blue Heaven*, Bess smiled. The song brought back good memories. She felt herself drawn to the source of the music. She stepped over to the piano where she found a white-haired man, lean as a stick, playing without any sheet music. He had a pleasant smile and was clearly lost in the moment. He peeked up at Bess and smiled. She was fascinated by how fast his arms moved and how his fingers pounded out the right notes with such vigor.

"I love that song," Bess grinned to the man playing the piano.

"Then feel free to dance," the man replied without even glancing in her direction.

Bess laughed at the suggestion, choosing to take a seat on a nearby couch instead. She smiled while she listened to the song, tapping her hand on her knee while the heel of her foot bounced on the floor. She sat back in the couch to get comfy. The second she shifted her weight, something jabbed her in the back. She turned in her seat, reached down between the cushions and pulled out a small black leather book.

"What's this?" she asked to no one in particular.

Her first thought was that the owner was close by. She turned to the piano player and held up her find. Happily playing, he nodded at what she held but appeared unconcerned about her discovery. She walked around the sitting room, showing a few ladies who simply shook their heads when she asked them if they owned it.

With no one claiming the book, she sat back down on the couch and stared at the book on her lap. After studying the black cover for a few seconds, she decided to open the book in hopes of finding a name. Perhaps, she reasoned, the owner would be revealed on the inside cover. Instead she was greeted with a surprising message on the first page.

I will never forget the faces of all the people I have killed.

Bess nearly dropped the book after reading that first line. She reread the words, took a deep breath and tried to stay calm. She scanned a few more sentences to give herself some context in which those words were written. After reading a few pages she quickly determined that what she was holding was a diary. The date at the top of each page indicated how many decades ago the words in the first entry were written. What she read gave her a disturbing feeling that the author of this diary had actually killed many people. It was also giving her a headache.

"My goodness," she sighed while she read the words again.

Bess quickly closed the book and looked around the room searching for the possible author of those horrible words. She stood and let her gaze linger on many faces, thinking that a killer's face would be quite easy to identify.

"Where are you?" she whispered.

She spotted one woman who had dozed off on a couch. She looked at the man playing the piano. He appeared to be having such a good time playing for other residents, he hardly seemed like the kind of person weighted down by guilt. One lady sitting across from Bess was reading a romance novel, her head filled with love given the broad smile on her face. With these three people to choose from, Bess walked over to the piano and showed her book to the piano player.

"I found this under a cushion," she explained, handing over the book.

"Good for you," the man replied while he continued to play. "You know what they say…finders keepers."

Bess glanced at the book, thinking this would be a find she'd rather not keep.

"Do you know who it belongs to?" she asked.

"No," the man quickly answered and a wide smile worked its way across his red cheeks after finishing a very difficult combination on the keys. "I'm only focused on my music this morning, not people. Would you like to hear a different song? I take requests!"

"Not right now," she sighed.

When he heard her answer, the man abruptly stopped, stood up from the piano and looked around. The room was empty except for Bess and a dozing resident on the couch.

"It looks like my audience has gone for the day," the man chirped.

With those final words, the piano player bowed once to Bess before leaving the room with the kind of brisk strut reminiscent of a performer leaving a stage. Bess couldn't help but smile at his theatrics and dramatic demeanor. As he left, two ladies entered the room, sat down and began a conversation about the heat outside. Bess could hear them mention the triple digit temperature, which made her glad to be in the air conditioning instead of walking to Dogwood Lane.

"Bess!" she heard a man's voice call out.

She turned around to see Chet standing by himself in the hallway. It appeared his impromptu meeting with Mutt was over. She glanced down at the book in her hand and thought briefly about stuffing it back under the cushion of the couch. However, her curiosity led her to tuck the book under her arm instead. She walked over to Chet.

"What did you find?" he asked, pointing at the book.

"I think it's some sort of diary," Bess softly replied before handing it to Chet for him to examine. "But...it's a very odd diary to read."

"Odd...how?" he asked.

"It's...hard for me to explain," Bess replied.

"So who does it belong to?" Chet asked.

"I found it under a cushion over there on that couch," she reported, pointing across the room.

"Then maybe we should give it to one of the nurses," he suggested.

"I don't think that would be wise," Bess quickly said, taking the diary from Chet and tucking it under her arm again.

"Why do you say that?" he asked.

"Because there's no name on this book," she replied. "I thought I'd borrow it for the afternoon and read through the pages to find some clues for an owner. There has to be a name on one of these pages. At least a first name. With any luck, I might be able find some clues and return it to the proper person. The nurses here aren't mind readers, Chet. They're too busy to make the effort to find the owner. You know they'll just tuck it in a drawer and forget all about it."

"True enough," Chet smiled, knowing full well it was impossible to control his wife's natural curiosity.

"Looks like you found yourself a little mystery to solve, Bess. Let's get back to our room so you can begin your investigation."

"A mystery to be solved in air conditioning," Bess smiled. "Now that's the best kind of mystery to investigate."

It was an unusual situation, Bess reflected. As a former police officer in her hometown of Venton, she had looked into many mysteries. She had solved many cases by travelling around, observing people, and finding clues in the most unusual places. This case was different. It was, to the best of her recollection, the first mystery that allowed her to sit down, prop up her feet and search for clues.

She started her investigation by sinking into Chet's favorite couch next to the bay window. While the light was good to read by, she found the warm sunshine pouring in through the windows grew hotter with each passing hour. Soon Bess was fanning herself with one hand while she read. Eventually it simply got too hot to stay there. She grabbed a cup of water and moved to a different chair away from the windows and resumed her search for clues.

For the next hour, she found herself absorbed by the passages she was studying. While she had yet to find the author's name, the emotion put into every line was absorbing. In fact, she was so focused on what she was reading that she was faintly aware of Chet sitting across from her working on a crossword puzzle.

With every page she turned, Bess began to realize that this was anything but a typical diary. At times, she couldn't even tell if the air conditioning was off or if her blood pressure was surging from some of the disturbing passages she was reading.

After studying the entries from morning through afternoon, it seemed to Bess that this was more than just a diary. It was almost a long painful series of confessions. A book of collected essays centered on the subject of sin and regret for committing those sins. Reading the book was like looking into someone's soul, she thought. The pages she reviewed were filled with stories, thoughts and anecdotes about the bad choices made in one life. From the many people the writer claimed to have killed, to an entry detailing how the writer struck his wife in a drunken rage, to another passage where he described getting fired from his job for punching his boss. It seemed like this was a diary written to unburden one's soul from a lifetime of wrongdoings and missteps. The more she read, the more Bess could tell there was a lot of unburdening. She could also tell that the burdens were born from a dark heart.

"Bess," Chet's voice spoke. "It's time for dinner."

As if waking from a trance, Bess looked up at Chet, blinked a few times and checked her watch. Much to her surprise, the hours had flown by. She put the book aside and followed Chet out the door and right to the elevator.

She was unusually quiet eating meat loaf and rice. She did not make any comments about her day. No anecdotal observations about the people sitting around them. Instead, she was lost in thought. Lost in the words she'd spent the afternoon reading. Lost in another person's memories of a difficult life.

"You're thinking about something," Chet said. "I can tell when you've got thoughts spinning around in your head. You have this expression you wear on your face."

"What expression?" Bess asked.

"It's like someone is testing you," Chet stated, his face suddenly changing to a somber expression. "Like someone is inside your head asking questions and you're working hard to answer them. You bite your bottom lip and you just stare at nothing."

Bess smiled, scooping up some rice from her plate and slipping it into her mouth.

"I'm sorry about that," she mumbled. "I was just thinking about what I read today."

"You mean that book?" he asked.

Bess nodded before putting another spoonful of rice in her mouth.

"I'm sorry I'm so quiet," she said.

"It's all right," Chet shrugged. "I like watching you work this way. Sometimes when you investigate a mystery you go off and I don't get to see much of you. At least for this mystery I can see the wheels turning while I enjoy my meat loaf and rice."

Bess smiled at her husband's sweet words before resuming her meal along with the many thoughts that swirled in her head. She thought about sharing all the disturbing things she read, but quickly reasoned that it made no sense to ruin Chet's meal.

The next morning, she found herself sitting with her friends in the Game Room, enjoying another meeting of Bridge Club. While the cards were dealt, Bess again was quiet and lost in her thoughts. She pondered the best way to broach the subject of what she had read the previous day. While she didn't share her thoughts with Chet, she felt differently about her friends. She'd known Alma, Rose and Flo for a long time. They were good friends and, if one thing were true in life, good friends were always the ones who lessened life's burdens. This diary had become a burden for Bess.

After some thought, she finally decided on the right words to use.

"Have any of you ever thought about the quality of people we live with here at the Honey Hills Center?"

"Define *quality*," Alma replied, her eyes locked on the cards she was holding.

"Whether they have a good heart or not," Bess suggested.

"Everyone seems fairly nice to me," Flo mumbled, laying down one card.

"I agree," Alma added.

"Why are you bringing this up?" Rose asked.

"Because," Bess began, then she sat back in her seat and drew in her breath while choosing her words carefully. "What if...um...I told you all something unpleasant."

"Are you sick?" Alma asked, leaning forward in her seat.

"No, no," Bess said with a wave of her hand. "I'm fine. It's just that, well, what if I told you something about our home here at the Honey Hills. What if I told you something that would change the way you look at this place?"

"Like what?" Flo asked. "We already know they're changing the name...which upsets some of us at this table. Me, I don't really care. So, I doubt there's anything else you can say that would upset me about this place."

Bess cleared her throat and looked at Flo.

"What if I told you...there's a killer living in our midst," Bess quietly stated.

The moment she spoke those words, she could sense the silence rushing around the table. She noticed that Flo's face dropped into an expression of surprise, which was rare for Flo. Alma's mouth was also hanging wide open. Rose was just glaring at Bess.

"Is there something more you would like to share, Bess?" Rose asked. "Saying something like that…there has to be more to it. I've lived here long enough to know they don't let criminals stay here."

"Yes," Flo nodded, and she looked around and leaned over the table. "Announcing there's a killer in our retirement home…and then growing silent…well that's not acceptable, Bess. You must give us more information. Who are you talking about?"

"I doubt it's anyone you know," Bess smiled.

"I'd still like to hear a name," Alma stated.

"I…I don't know a name," Bess replied, looking around at each face. "All I know is it may be a resident here at the Honey Hills. I also suspect this person has killed people in the past."

Again, silence greeted her words. Rose, Flo and Alma all leaned forward on their elbows and stared at Bess, who was fiddling with her playing cards.

"Is that it?" Flo asked, her voice growing sharper.

"Keep your voice down," Alma said, standing up and closing the door to the Game Room. "Other residents don't need to hear us talking about such things."

"Let me get this straight," Rose finally spoke. "Are you telling us that someone who lives in this retirement home, a fellow resident, is a killer?"

"That's what I believe," Bess stated.

"How can you be so sure?" Alma asked.

"Because I've come into possession of a rather disturbing…diary," Bess began. "I found a small black journal underneath the cushion of a sofa near the multi-purpose room. I don't know who it belongs to, but the passages I've read provide accounts of some very disturbing memories. As a matter of fact, right there on the first page is a sentence about regrets over killing people."

"Killing people?" Flo grunted.

"My gosh!" Alma said, nearly dropping her cards on the table.

"That sounds very strange to me," Rose softly offered.

"Should we call the police?" Flo asked.

"I thought about it," Bess nodded. "However, I took all day yesterday and read this diary from cover to cover. It's my belief that these terrible events occurred a long time ago. No one here in our retirement home has been murdered...or is in any danger of being murdered."

"Thank goodness," Alma sighed.

"In my opinion," Bess continued, "this person, the author of the diary, hasn't killed anyone for many years. What I can imply from the passages I read is that the writer is a man who, I believe, was a soldier in a war. Like all young men in a war, he found himself in situations where he had to kill enemy soldiers in combat. From what I read, the memories and the scars run deep for him. At least that's what the passages I read imply."

"So these killings were committed...when he was in a war?" Alma asked.

"That's what I believe," Bess nodded.

"I still find all of this...unsettling," Alma stated, massaging her forehead.

"I feel sympathetic for that man," Flo mumbled.

"Sympathy?" Alma asked. "Why would you feel that way about someone who took another person's life?"

Flo cleared her throat and placed her cards down on the table.

"When I was a girl," Flo began, "I remember how my father would wake in the middle of the night yelling about shooting the enemy and my mother would always have to calm him down and put me back to bed. A few years later, when I was older, my father told me stories about killing young German men during the war. They were stories that gave me nightmares because I wasn't even a teenager. Killing those young men was a burden my father carried with him until the day he died. His dreams just...haunted him."

"Taking a human life *should* be an unforgettable burden," Ruth surmised.

"I agree," Alma nodded, pointing across the table to Ruth. "Life is precious. I think it shows that the writer of that diary is a good person for regretting the lives that were taken. I'd be more concerned about the person who doesn't value human life all that much. Someone who takes a life and then simply forgets about it."

"Good point," Ruth said, nodding to Alma's words. "And what do you think, Bess? I mean you're the one who found this...diary. You're the one reading it. Do you have an opinion on the passages you've been reading? Are you comfortable with this resident calling the Honey Hills their home?"

Bess lowered her cards and glanced around the table.

"In my mind," Bess began, "whenever I see the face of a fellow resident I always like to think the best of them. On the surface, we're all sweet older people simply occupying our days here. Sometimes it's easy to forget that there is more to us under the surface. At our age, we are people who have led full lives filled with mistakes both big and small. We all have said and done things that others might not agree with. We all try to present a pleasant side to others, but in the end...we are what God made us. We are flawed. To expect otherwise from ourselves, or others, is simply not a fair standard, in my opinion."

"So what are you going to do about that diary?" Alma asked.

"Yes," Rose nodded, "there are so many people living here at the Honey Hills Center. It would be hard for anyone to figure out who the owner is."

Bess shifted in her seat and remained silent for a few seconds.

"I think this calls for a process of elimination," Bess said, leaning forward in her seat and placing her cards on the table. "Let's begin by discussing what is known. Judging from what I've read...I know it's a man. Given what he's written about the people he killed...I suspect him to be a war veteran. If that's the case, the Honey Hills Center designates a Veteran's Room with a gold star above the door. It's a room for veterans to meet and talk about their experiences. That would be a good place to start."

"Yes, that's a good start," Alma nodded. "Anything else to distinguish the author from the many veterans we have living here?"

"His handwriting," Bess continued. "Judging by the style of handwriting in the book I'd be willing to bet the man I'm looking for is left handed."

"How could you possibly know that?" Flo asked.

"By the direction that the letters in the journal are slanted," Bess replied. "My brother was left handed and when he was in high school he was always bending his arm and his wrist a certain way to get his letters to look like other students who were right handed. When he got older, my brother just didn't care anymore. His name was always slanted more to the left than to the right...like the entries in this journal."

"A very good observation," Alma grinned. "You really are good at noticing the little things, Bess."

"Thank you," Bess replied.

"Do you have any other clues?" Rose asked.

"On one page the author refers to going to a state fair in Lincoln a few times," she reported. "He also wrote that he met his wife in Lincoln. Then in one passage he even talked about fond memories of attending the University of Nebraska football games. I'd be willing to guess Lincoln, Nebraska, is where this man grew up."

"So to sum up," Rose stated, sitting up a little straighter in her seat. "You're looking for a man who may be a war veteran. A man who is left handed and may have been raised in or around Lincoln, Nebraska. Anything else?"

"I think that's it," Bess smiled.

"Well, good luck with that!" Flo laughed, picking up her cards and examining them. "Now onto more pressing matters, ladies. For me, that means looking to win my first round of bridge this morning."

At that moment, everyone examined the cards they were dealt. The words ceased. Focus garnered the table and another round of bridge was underway. For Bess, the game was now a bit more enjoyable. Her burden had been shared.

Chapter 19: THE SEARCH FOR A KILLER

The Honey Hills Retirement community is a large compound. Occupied by a few hundred retirees, Bess often thought it would be impossible for one person to know the names of every resident who called Honey Hills their home. While she was well aware of the scope of her suspects, she also knew that she could whittle that large number down when she considered the veterans who lived there. One thing she thought of was trying to meet as many veterans as she could. In doing this, it would give her the opportunity to shake hands, talk to them and narrow her scope. It would be a large undertaking, but Bess was ready for the challenge, especially since it kept her in the main building.

First, she'd have to make a change in her routine. Since moving into the Tranquil Tower, Bess had spent most of her time with Chet. Now she'd have to leave her fancy room every morning and start being more outgoing and more social.

Every morning she set out from her room to chat with nurses about the veterans in the main building. Whenever she did this, she'd always state that she was looking for veterans in the main building to thank them for their service. Most of the nurses she spoke to were delighted by her gesture and happy to help Bess fulfill her request.

Over the next couple of days, she met and spoke with a great deal of veterans. She usually skipped the rooms where a woman was a vet, simply because she knew a woman was not the author of the diary.

When she'd arrive at a room, Bess would typically introduce herself and ask for the veteran by name. Upon meeting the veteran, Bess would introduce herself and state her reason for her visit. She'd go on to express some words of thanks for the veteran's service, which was always welcomed with a smile and a lengthy discourse. Most visits were positive. Some residents gave her lots of details about their service. Some, Bess found, were more reluctant to open up.

After every visit, she'd always make a point of shaking hands with the veteran to see if they shook with their left hand or their right. The visit required patience and close attention to detail. Carrying a pen and small notecard, Bess would carefully record the names of every left-handed veteran she met. After a week, she had a small list of names to study.

One morning, she was pondering her list of left-handed veterans when she heard a knock on the door. She glanced at her watch and sighed.

"Ten o'clock," Bess grumbled and she rolled her eyes.

A knock on the door at ten o'clock was part of the routine that came with moving to the Honey Hills main building. It was also a daily reminder of her mortality. Every morning a nurse was assigned to knock on the door to every resident's apartment. The knock usually came at around ten o'clock in the morning. Bess called it "the death knock." She gave it that title because she thought it was the nurse's way of verifying all the residents made it through another night's sleep. If someone didn't answer the door, Bess thought, the nurse was certain to find a dead body on the other side. At least that was Bess's theory.

"Sounds like the death knock," Chet observed from behind the newspaper he was reading. He lowered his newspaper and grinned at Bess. "Shall I open it and disappoint them by showing that we're still breathing."

"Hush," Bess grinned back, waving her hand for good measure. "It's part of their job, Chet. Be nice."

She walked across the room and opened the door.

"Good morning," Bess smiled to a young nurse who worked on her floor.

"Morning, Bess," the young nurse shot back in between chewing her gum and handing her a small paper cup with some medicine in it. "Here are your pills for today. How did you and your husband sleep?"

"Very well," Bess replied, taking the medicine and glancing in at the two familiar pills that greeted her every day.

"Here's some water," the young girl said, handing her another paper cup.

"Thank you," Bess said before quickly digesting the medication with what little water she was given. "What is today's date?"

"It's the first of July," the nurse replied. "Hard to believe we're only going into July. May and June were so warm. I hope this summer doesn't get much hotter."

"I agree," Bess nodded. "I have a question I was hoping you could answer."

"I can try," the young nurse smiled.

"You know, in the past the Honey Hills Center has always a had a lovely July 4th picnic to thank our veterans for their service," Bess began. "Now, as you noted, we're in the midst of a hot summer. Given this heat wave, do you know if they would cancel the picnic? I think it would be terribly uncomfortable to have it outside."

"I heard they're going to do it in the evening this year," the nurse explained. "I saw some people setting up tents in the courtyard. There should be plenty of shade for everyone who attends, since the sun will be lower in the sky."

"And hopefully a breeze," Bess nodded. "Do you think they would cancel the picnic if it got too hot? Even with the tents?"

"I think they'd just back it up a day or two," the nurse replied. "After all, it's called a *Veteran's Picnic*. We would like the evening to be comfortable so lots of veterans will attend. After all, we invited a band. We have sparklers. We want it to be a festive event. Even Reid Collins will be there."

"Who?" Bess asked.

"He's our State Representative," the nurse replied.

"I see," Bess smiled. "Whenever they decide to hold it I do hope it won't be too hot. After all, nobody likes to see a politician sweat."

The nurse laughed at Bess's joke and stepped into the hallway.

"Keep your fingers crossed for good weather," the nurse advised with a wink of her eye before walking to the next room.

Bess closed the door and walked into the kitchen area. She glanced over to Chet, who was absorbed in a crossword puzzle.

"It will be helpful to have all the veterans together," she said to herself.

She quietly walked into her bedroom, sat down on her bed and grabbed the diary from her nightstand. The dark leather cover felt rough in the palm of her hand. She leaned back on the couch, sipped some water and cracked open the diary. She quietly reviewed a few pages that she had read the night before. Then she turned to a new page and read a few more entries. After a couple of minutes, she closed the book.

"Such a sad life," she sighed.

She stood up and stepped over to a window. She stared out at the grounds that made up the Honey Hills community. She spotted two ladies out walking in the heat. She stepped closer to the window, adjusted her bifocals, but didn't recognize the women. Her mind quickly began to center on how she felt about sharing the main building with so many residents that she didn't know.

More specifically, she never gave much thought to the journey each of the residents had taken on their way to living at the Honey Hills. What joys they celebrated in their lives. What disappointments they endured. What sins they committed. It was something she never gave much thought to…until she found the diary. Reading such depressing entries caused her to reflect on the quality of the people she saw every day. It also made her wary of the lifelong burdens that some of them carried.

Chapter 20: JULY 4th

Two days came and went. Having studied every page of the diary for more clues, Bess decided to stop. It was just too depressing to finish. The pages she read only laid out more sins and more mistakes brought on by alcohol and a bad temper. After studying a few more pages, there appeared to be no additional clues as to the identity of the author. Now more than ever, she was counting on the picnic to gather her suspects together and find the left-handed veteran who lost this book.

On the morning of July 4th Bess stepped outside more than once throughout the day to survey the temperature. On her morning walk, she was pleased to find the air slightly cooler than the previous morning. She also noted a slight northern breeze, which in Pennsylvania meant a relief from the oppressive humid air.

By the afternoon, Bess learned that the picnic was scheduled to begin on time. After dinner, she found herself standing outside with Chet at seven o'clock. They stood beneath the shade of a large oak tree. They were two of many residents who gathered in a large courtyard surrounded by the main building. A pair of large white tents were located at the center of the courtyard. In between the tents was a small stage where a band played.

It was a warm evening, but not as oppressively hot as the previous days. The north wind she felt in the morning, was indeed bringing more agreeable air.

Because of the comfortable temperatures, she was surprised at how many residents decided to come out to enjoy the festivities and honor their veterans. Most of the men and women in attendance were seated on chairs, under the shade from the tents, waving small American flags while the band filled the courtyard with patriotic songs.

"I'm going to walk around a little," Bess told Chet, who was happily clapping his hands to the music.

With each step, Bess carefully took in every detail and every person. She noticed the clothes being worn. She studied the expressions on each face. She counted the number of veterans in attendance and even managed to spot a few who were using their left hands to eat a hotdog or drink a cup of lemonade. In walking around, she overheard more than a few conversations. When she completed one lap through each tent, she returned to where Chet was standing and enjoying the band.

"I got us some lemonade from the refreshment tent," Chet stated, handing her a paper cup.

"Thank you," Bess said, downing the small portion with one gulp while trying not to notice how warm it tasted in her mouth.

"I think the band sounds splendid," Chet observed, glancing up to the small makeshift stage. Bess smiled at the four-man band. A trumpet, the drums, a baritone and a banjo were all that was needed to entertain the crowd. She marveled at how these unlikely instruments complemented each other in making perfect harmony for many patriotic tunes. Suddenly, Chet stepped in front of Bess and bounced on his toes while holding her hand.

"C'mon, Twinkle Toes, let's dance!" Chet grinned.

"No, Chet!" Bess scolded, pulling her hand away. "You know I don't like being the center of attention.

You might enjoy dancing in front of all these people but not me."

"Maybe I'll just have to dance by myself," Chet grinned, letting go of her hand before swinging his hips like a hula dancer.

Bess didn't crack a smile. She had a purpose for attending this picnic and it wasn't to dance. Her eyes turned to the crowd, looking for uniforms or hats or anything to signify a veteran in attendance. She counted nearly a hundred residents moving around the spacious yard, some getting food or drinks while others were happily seated in the shade of two large trees. Feeling some sweat forming on her face, Bess left Chet to step under the shade of a tent.

Once in the shade, she grabbed another cup of lemonade. Sipping a cooler serving, she moved carefully around to observe the residents seated under the tent. Among the many residents she spotted were four veterans, all dressed in their uniforms, seated close to the stage. She continued to walk around, spotting some more veterans under the tent.

Suddenly she spied one veteran who was drinking with his left hand. He had a full thick head of white hair, sitting by himself, staring up at the stage. What caught her eye was how his face held no expression. Given the festive setting, she found his glum face an oddity. Her curiosity was piqued. As she approached, she could tell he was taller and heavier than she was. If this was her suspect, a small part of her wished she had taken up boxing all those years ago.

"Excuse me," Bess said stepping next to the veteran. She held the diary up with one hand and thought of the best fib she could muster. "I found this lying on the ground. Did you drop it?"

The man tipped up his sunglasses, glanced down at the book in her hand, and shook his head with the same grim expression riding his face. He grunted something she didn't understand and walked away.

"That went well," Bess sighed.

She turned around and let her eyes linger on the crowd packed into the courtyard. Her eyes considered all the details that presented themselves to her. Those people who were seated and those who were standing. The expressions on the faces. Those who spoke to friends and those who preferred to stand or sit by themselves.

Suddenly, the band began to play the national anthem which brought the crowd to their feet. Bess turned to the stage and watched as a veteran, dressed in full uniform, carried in a flag and stood in front of the gathering. With melodic voices filling the air, Bess did not allow herself to get caught up in the moment. Her eyes weren't on the flag. Instead, they were on the people around her. She looked at the number of men and women who stood with hands above their brow, saluting the flag. The music gave her the perfect opportunity to sort through the crowd. She spotted some faces she knew from her visits to veterans' rooms. A few faces she knew from taking her walks. Even some faces that she recognized from the Dining Hall. When the music stopped, she watched them all sit down.

"Did you spot anyone interesting?" Chet asked.

"Not yet," Bess replied, her eyes glancing around the yard. "I'm afraid I'm not very good at having a short time span for finding a suspect, Chet."

"What do you mean?" he asked.

"I've found plenty of left handed veterans here," Bess stated. "They just don't appear to be what I'm looking for. I can't explain it. They just don't...*feel* right to me. In fact, none of these people appear to be who I'm looking for. None of them have the right…look. Maybe I'm losing my powers of observation. I'm sure that happens with old age. I hate to say it, Chet, but right now…I'm feeling a bit stuck."

"You're what?" Chet asked, looking at the band instead of her.

"I said I'm stuck," Bess said a little louder.

"I don't understand," Chet said, stepping closer to her. He took her hands and moved her like they were dancing. "You're just not hearing the music, Bess. See? Your feet are moving. You're clearly not stuck."

"I'm not talking about my feet," Bess said, pulling Chet's hand off her waist and gesturing back to the veterans. "Look at these people. I came here this evening with the firm belief that one of these veterans is the owner of this book. One of them has to be. I've looked them all over from head to toe…but I just can't figure out which one is the author. My instincts aren't pointing me to anyone in particular. In fact, I'd say right now my instincts are taking the evening off. Perhaps who I'm looking for just isn't here."

"Let me help you with that," Chet grinned.

In one swift motion, Chet snatched the diary from her hands, hopped up on the small stage in front of the band and grabbed the microphone. Bess was petrified.

"What is he doing?" she mumbled.

He looked so natural being the center of attention, Bess thought. However, she also noticed that the members of the band were looking quite confused over her husband's action. He turned to the band, gestured for them to stop playing a song, then turned back to the audience and smiled.

"Chet! Come back here!" Bess called out and she took one step towards the stage but it was too late. Like it or not, her husband was determined to help.

"Good evening ladies and gentlemen!" Chet spoke into the microphone.

The people gathered in the courtyard stopped talking and looked at Chet. It looked like they weren't quite sure what was happening. Some in the crowd clapped. Some just stared. Bess could feel a headache coming on and she began to rub her forehead.

"A happy Fourth of July to one and all!" Chet grinned and he gestured to Bess. "My name is Chet Wooden. Some of you know me from Waltzing Club...which is a fine club to belong to if you like to dance. On behalf of the Waltzing Club, my wife and I would like to thank all of our veterans for their service today. I would also like to thank any spouses for the sacrifices they had to make for family members to serve."

Chet paused and Bess could tell he wasn't quite sure what to say next. The crowd was silent, some without expression and some smiling. Chet cleared his throat, then lifted the diary high in the air.

"When we were coming to this wonderful event my wife found this little journal on the floor of a sitting room in the main building," Chet continued. "It appears to be a diary written by a veteran. I read a few pages but couldn't find the name of the owner."

"You shouldn't read someone's diary!" a woman's voice called out.

"Like I said, I was looking for the name of the book's owner," Chet replied and he forced a smile. "I promise you I didn't read much. Now if this book belongs to any of you, please raise your hand so I can return it."

Chet lowered the microphone and looked around for any movement. He continued to hold the small book up high for all to see. Bess also looked around, as did most of the people in attendance. After a few seconds, it was clear that no one was standing up. In fact, it appeared to Bess that everyone was quite still, sweating, and whispering to each other in the midst of this awkward moment created by her well-meaning husband. When it was clear that no one was going to claim the book, Chet offered an uncomfortable smile in reply to the silence.

"Okay, then," Chet mumbled before stepping away from the microphone. He waved the book in the air one more time and nodded as he stepped off the stage. All eyes followed him as he walked through the courtyard to where Bess was standing. She could feel every eye focus on her, but she refused to return their gaze. Chet handed Bess the diary.

"Unstuck, yet?" he asked.

"Thank you, Chet," Bess sighed, gently placing her hand in his. "While I appreciate your thoughtfulness to help...a little more discretion would have been appreciated."

"You know me," Chet grinned. "I like to jump right in with both feet."

"That's why you're such a good dancer," Bess smiled.

The band began to play and the murmurs in the crowd slowly diminished. Soon every eye had turned away from Chet and Bess and back to the band. People resumed their walk to the snack bars for hotdogs and lemonade. Bess wiped some sweat from her forehead and thought about getting another cup of lemonade.

"Excuse me," a soft voice spoke from behind Bess's left shoulder.

Bess and Chet both turned to see a short, narrow woman with dark hair, glasses and a rather sharp looking chin that angled down to her chest.

"That diary you were talking about...that belongs to me," the woman said, pointing to the journal.

Bess could feel her eyebrows go down, as they often did when something caught her off guard.

"You mean this diary?" Bess asked, holding it up. "You're talking about *this* diary?"

"I recognize the cover...and the size," the woman replied.

Bess stepped between Chet and the woman and held the diary up.

"I've read this more than my husband," Bess began. "From what I've learned, a woman didn't write these passages. This diary belongs to a man. And, if I recall correctly, he's a very happy man who has led a long good life."

"Happy?" the woman asked, and she nervously folded her arms over her chest. "I'm sorry, but I must have made a mistake. While it looks familiar to me, the diary I'm thinking of is by no means a happy one."

Bess slowly nodded.

"You're right," Bess said. "I'm sorry for the fib, but I had to be sure it's your book. As I said, I've spent more than a few nights reading this diary. When I read the first passage, the part about killing people...it just made me curious to read more. I'm a former police officer and my curious nature gets the better of me sometimes. There are many sad things written in this diary, but, of course, you already know that."

The woman reached out and took the diary from Bess's hand. She held it up to her face, slowly running her thumbs over the black bumpy cover.

"So you read my husband's journal?" she asked.

"Yes," Bess nodded, looking over the woman's shoulder for a veteran to approach them. "Where is your husband?"

"He's not out here," the woman replied. "If you'd like, I can introduce him to both of you. Come with me and I'll take you right to him."

Given the heat, and her overwhelming curiosity, it was an invitation that Bess could not refuse.

Chapter 21: THE KILLER CONCEALED

When they entered the main building, Bess felt an agreeable sigh leave her lips. The crisp air conditioning even caused her to smile a little the moment she and Chet followed the woman through the entrance.

"I'm sorry," Bess said, turning to the woman. "All that heat has caused me to forget my manners. I forgot to introduce myself. My name is Bess Bullock. This is my husband, Chet. What is your name?"

"Mildred Bentz," the woman replied, glancing over her shoulder just enough to allow Chet and Bess to catch a snapshot of her profile.

"So...where are we going?" Bess asked.

"I told you we're going to meet my husband," she explained.

Together they turned a corner, Chet nearly bumping into one nurse.

"My wife found this diary nearly a week ago buried in a couch," Chet reported, pointing to the small book Mildred was carrying. "Has your husband been missing it?"

Mildred remained silent.

"Like I said, I read a lot of his entries," Bess spoke up. "While I didn't find an actual name, I did come across some very troubling passages. Your husband has had a lot of pain in his life, Mrs. Bentz."

These words caused her to stop. She turned and looked directly at Bess.

"We *both* have had a great deal of pain," Mildred replied, her eyes narrowing. "You see, when we were engaged, my husband was the sweetest man. Always brought me flowers and wrote me poems. Then he was drafted to serve in the army. We married when he came home after basic training and then he shipped out. I didn't see him for a year. When he returned from the war, there were no services to help him cope with what he experienced. All they told him was to try to go off and lead a normal life."

"A *normal* life is easier said than done," Bess remarked.

The conversation went no farther. Mildred resumed her walk with Bess and Chet trailing behind. They followed Mildred down one hall, around a corner and down another long corridor. Together the threesome moved deeper into the main building. Soon Bess recognized one hallway which led to the dementia wing. Mildred stopped at the entrance and typed a code into a keypad mounted to the wall. The double doors leading to the dementia unit unlocked and opened.

"Follow me," she instructed.

Bess had been to the dementia wing before to visit friends. It was the only part of the main building that made her feel uneasy. It wasn't because she was afraid of the residents who lived there. On the contrary, it was the recognition that at one point those residents who suffered from dementia were normal functioning retirees. Then, without warning, their minds just changed. It was a common fear among a lot of people Bess knew.

The fear of having one's mind give out before the body was ready to follow.

"Over here," Mildred said, waving them to a large room with full windows facing a courtyard. At the center of the room were a few dementia patients sitting in wheelchairs. They were positioned in a circle with a nurse in the middle, tossing a small beach ball to each person. Bess knew this was a typical activity used to stimulate the brains of some patients. Mildred bypassed that group and continued to walk over to a bald headed man sitting by himself in a wheelchair. He was facing a window that had a lovely view of some horses in a nearby field.

"Hello, sweetheart," Mildred whispered.

Bess and Chet watched her lean over and kiss the smooth top of his bald head. There was no response from him. While he stared out the window, Bess studied his face. He had patches of white stubble around the sides of his cheeks and along his chin. He had round glasses and deep blue eyes that were fixed on the window. Slowly, Bess saw the man's blue eyes turn when Mildred grabbed his hand. He looked at her hand, turned to her face and smiled. The expression on his face softened and his mouth tried to form a slight smile.

"Look, Sam, these nice people came to see you," Mildred said to her husband. "They found something that was lost."

She gently placed Sam Bentz's diary on his lap. He instinctively reached over with one hand, picked up the book and held it close to his chest. It reminded Bess of how a child would use one hand to hold a teddy bear. Perhaps, she thought, there was some security for Sam in holding that book.

His blue eyes narrowed and the expression on his face grew rigid again when he looked at Chet and Bess. It was clearly an expression born from a suspicious heart. At first, Bess found the gaze unsettling, but then she reasoned that the expression was one of mistrust. After all, she thought, if she had placed her deepest darkest secrets in a diary and thought other people were reading those secrets wouldn't she also have the right to be angry? Somehow that diary cut right through the dementia and directly into his heart, she observed.

"Mr. Bentz," Bess began, pulling up a chair and sitting across from him. "I found your diary by accident. My husband and I were quite fortunate to meet your wife so we could return it to you."

Mr. Bentz's eyes remained locked on his diary. He grunted and it sounded to Bess like he was trying to speak, but the words were too muddled to understand. Bess also noticed how his other hand reached out and also came to rest on the book's cover.

Bess turned to Mildred.

"It's clear to me that he really values this book," Bess began. "My only question to you is how could he be so careless in losing it? Especially under the cushion of a couch outside of *this* dementia unit? I don't understand how that could happen? If he's a patient in this wing, I know they always keep the doors locked for the safety of the patients. So I'm not quite sure how he managed to slip out...do you?"

Mildred looked down at her husband and gently ran one hand over his head.

"I don't think *he* lost it," Bess whispered.

"When you found the book," Mildred began in a soft voice, "you said you read a good many of the entries, didn't you?"

"I read a few pages," Bess fibbed.

"Then you've read enough to know this is a book of painful recollections," Mildred explained. "You see, Mrs. Bullock, my husband had a lot of pain in his life. Before he fought in a war we were a young happy couple. The things that war did to him...it just shouldn't be allowed. If there were any justice, they'd simply wipe away those horrible memories from my dear husband so I could have the man I married back again."

"So he suffered after serving in the war?" Bess asked.

"*We* suffered," Mildred nodded. "Me, my children and my husband. It was a struggle to keep our marriage together. The passages in that book are so painful to me...I don't even want to read them. Just looking at that old worn cover, it's enough to make my heart race and my stomach turn."

"You must have been happy to lose it," Bess suggested and she glanced down at Sam.

"Out of sight...out of mind. Isn't that what they say?"

Mildred remained silent.

"Of course," Bess observed, turning her eyes back to Mildred, "your husband is locked in here. As I mentioned, there's no way he could escape with that book. The nurses monitor that door like hawks. So, in my opinion, how that diary left this facility is indeed a mystery."

Bess stared at Mildred in hopes that she would clear the air on this matter. Mildred blinked once and looked down at her hands.

Bess took one measured step closer to Mildred.

"I know it was you," Bess softly stated.

The words caused Mildred to look down at her husband and gently run her hand over his shoulder.

"One day, after visiting Sam," Mildred began, "I was having a terrible day. I was walking the hallways crying and thinking about all the pain that war had brought into my life. I was wiping away tears with each step. Then I thought about that book. I hated all the memories it contained. I hated how it was a constant reminder of our sad life. I don't know why he holds onto it. Lose the book and lose the pain...that's what I told myself."

"So you acted on that thought?" Bess asked.

"I took the book with me after I visited him," Mildred nodded. "I waited until Sam was sleeping and then I took it from the nightstand in his room. I carried it around with me for most of the day thinking about how I could dispose of it. I lingered by more than one trash can, debating about whether to toss it in. Then I walked down to a sitting room, sat down and listened to someone play a piano. The music was so sad, and I was holding that book, and I just wanted to get rid of it as fast as I could. That's when I shoved it under that cushion and walked away. Like a dog burying a bone I'd suppose. Leaving that book behind just felt like…feeling the weather change from clouds and rain to sunshine. For the next couple of days I felt better without that diary."

"Until I found it," Bess nodded.

Mildred looked at Bess and turned her eyes to Sam.

"When you stood up on that stage this morning," Mildred explained, pointing to Chet. "When you stood there waving that book in the air…I just didn't want to stand up. I didn't want to claim it. After a few minutes…I knew the right thing to do was to get it back for Sam. He has trouble speaking but…I could tell he missed having his diary."

"I'm certain claiming that diary was hard for you to do," Bess replied. "After you went to all the trouble of getting rid of it…I think it says something about your love for your husband. You could have very easily sat in that courtyard and not said a word."

Mildred turned to her husband and rubbed his shoulder with her hand.

"I knew he wanted it back," she sighed. "He can't speak…but he can gesture. When I visited him after I hid that diary I could tell he missed it. He didn't say it of course…but I could tell. A wife always knows. In a strange way, the darkness in that book seems to provide some security for him…though I don't know why."

She turned her eyes to her husband who was staring down at the diary on his lap.

"So when I saw your husband on that stage…waving that book in the air…I knew I had to claim it," Mildred stated, resting her hand on her husband's hand. "You see, the dementia has taken away my Sam's ability to read. He has trouble speaking, too. He understands what I tell him and can still walk around and do things. Despite his dementia, there is something deep in him that knows this book is important, but I doubt he'll remember why. Right, my love?"

Sam let out a grunt in reply, his bright blue eyes staring straight ahead.

Bess said nothing. She stood and watched Mildred take her husband's hand and gently lace her slender fingers between his. She kissed him on the forehead and his eyes looked at her and his lips puckered together like he was kissing the air. It was clear to Bess that beneath the effects of his dementia, beneath the pain of war, there was still genuine love for his wife.

As Mildred stood beside Sam holding his hand, there appeared to be a sense of calm that came over his face. When he looked at his wife the features on his face relaxed. The book, or Mildred, seemed to provide some security. The way he looked at his wife, Bess thought, he didn't appear to be confused. There was something familiar and loving in his wife's company. Even though they lived in separate parts of the Honey Hills Center, he still remembered her. Like the luckiest married couples, home was not defined by a street or a location. It wasn't measured by the size of the walls or the yard. In this case, home was defined by a warm familiar place. For Sam Bentz, that place was somewhere in his wife's eyes.

Chapter 22: FIRE IN THE TREES

The next morning, Bess got a phone call from Anita Mackley. Bess hadn't spoken to Anita in quite a while and was prepared for her to demand details on Bess's ongoing investigation into her missing diamonds. Instead, Bess was pleasantly surprised when Anita cut right to the chase by volunteering to help with the case. Anita went on to suggest that they go down to spy on some of the workers on Dogwood Lane. While this wasn't Bess's style of observation and detection, she agreed to the idea to appease Anita.

An hour later, Bess found herself outside, following Anita away from the main building and down Magnolia Lane. It was later in the morning than Bess would have liked, but they thought it best to squeeze in the trip between breakfast and lunch. Unfortunately, leaving later in the morning also meant the sun was going to be hotter. Bess wiped the sweat from her face more than once during their walk. The air felt muggy and it was hard for her to take a deep breath.

"I wish we would have left earlier," Bess called out. "When I take a walk in the morning I notice that an hour makes a difference between a cool walk and a hot one."

"I agree," Anita replied, "it is very warm."

"How did you slip out without your husband being suspicious?" Bess asked.

"He was still asleep," Anita replied. "He was out late last night with a group of friends playing poker. I don't know if he lost any money...but he was tired this morning."

"Well, then let's get going before he wakes up," Bess grinned.

As she followed Anita down the street, Bess began to slow her pace. She noticed Anita was now walking farther and farther ahead of her. Suddenly, Bess stopped and rubbed her eyes. She looked around and noticed something odd. To one side of the road, she spotted a row of tall oak trees. The more she stared at the trees, the more she thought they didn't look quite right to her.

The longer she stared at the trees the more it appeared that they held an odd set of sparkling lights that were tucked deep in the branches. It was almost like someone lit candles that were flickering in the darkest recesses of the tree.

"What is that?" she whispered to herself.

When Bess got closer to the trees, she squinted but couldn't find any candles or fireflies to explain what she was seeing. She kept walking closer, with one eye on the flickering trees she was passing. In her mind, she simply couldn't determine the reason for what she was seeing.

A few more steps down the road, Bess had another strange experience. She began to feel like her feet were no longer touching the ground. She felt like she was somehow floating in the air. She stopped walking, closed her eyes and rubbed her forehead. The sweat filled her hand. She took a deep breath of humid air and tried to clear her head. She knew they were close to Dogwood Lane, but despite being so close to her home, Bess didn't feel like taking another step. She stopped in her tracks and continued to rub her forehead.

"Bess!" Anita called out and she turned back to where Bess was standing. "Bess! Are you feeling okay? What's the matter?"

"I...I don't know!" Bess called back. She stepped off the road and slowly began to lower herself into the grass. "I'm feeling a bit...lightheaded. It's like I'm dizzy...but I'm not. Things just don't look right to me."

Anita quickly walked back and grabbed Bess by the arm, helping to ease her into a sitting position on a slight hill.

"Is it a heart attack?" Anita asked, her voice growing louder.

"I never had one before," Bess replied. "I don't know what's happening to me."

"Does your chest hurt?" Anita asked.

"Nothing hurts," Bess said, rubbing her hands on the grass. "I just feel...funny."

"Well, you can't just sit out here," Anita advised, putting her hands on her hips and looking around. "It's just too hot to lounge in the grass. Can you walk back to the main building with me?"

"I don't think I can," Bess replied. "I...I feel kind of dizzy...too dizzy to walk."

"Then wait here," Anita instructed, pointing over to a worker cutting a hedge. "I'm going to go over there and get that groundskeeper. Maybe he has a radio to call for someone to come and help you. Are you okay if I do that?"

"I think I feel better sitting than standing," Bess said, waving one hand in the air. "Please go ahead and ask him to get some help. I'll be fine."

Anita promptly set off, leaving Bess in the grass. She squinted up at the hot sun, then the flickering trees, then she chose to shut her eyes. She could feel the heat from the sun beating down on the back of her neck with each minute that passed. She measured her breathing and tried to remain calm. She prayed that she would feel better and that someone would soon arrive to help.

A few minutes later, she heard the sound of an engine humming from up the road. She opened her eyes to see a small white truck accelerating around the corner. It roared up Magnolia Lane, pulled into the grass by the side of the road and parked next to where Bess was seated.

She quickly recognized the nurse who hopped out. Carrying a small black bag and kneeling in the grass next to Bess, Nurse Lucy was coming to the rescue. While she didn't know too many of the new nurses, Bess remembered Lucy because she had curly red hair that hung around her shoulders like the famous actress Lucille Ball.

"Hello, Mrs. Bullock," Nurse Lucy began, grabbing Bess by the wrist and checking her pulse. "You having a bad morning? Did you fall?"

"No," Bess replied. "I was just feeling dizzy and needed to sit down. I feel better when I sit, but things still look a little funny to me when I try to stand up."

"She just stopped here and dropped to the grass," Anita reported.

"I see," the nurse said, checking and pressing different parts of Bess's body. "Are you in any pain?"

"No," Bess quickly said.

"And when is the last time you had something to drink?" the nurse asked, grabbing Bess's wrist and checking her pulse.

"Drink?" Bess asked, "I had a little grape juice this morning."

"Anita Mackley tells me you've been taking a lot of walks in this heat," Nurse Lucy replied. "Weren't you at the July 4th picnic, too?"

"Yes," Bess said.

"Your vitals seem pretty good," Nurse Lucy said, letting go of Bess's wrist. "I'm going to take you back to the main building so we can get you in bed and check a few things out. Do you think we can help you climb in the truck?"

"I think so," Bess said, mustering herself out of the grass.

The moment she stood, Bess could feel her head begin to spin again. She grabbed Nurse Lucy with one hand while Anita grabbed Bess around the waist. Bess steadied herself on the truck door with the other hand, and managed to slide her narrow frame into the passenger seat. Once inside, she pulled the door shut and closed her eyes again.

"Feel better, Bess," Anita said, wiping either sweat or tears from her cheeks.

Bess nodded and closed her eyes. She tried to focus her mind on the sound of the engine for about a minute. She briefly wondered if Anita would continue on to Dogwood Lane or not. Bess tried to open her eyes, felt dizzy and closed them again.

As far as her health was concerned, Bess had led a charmed life. For more than eighty years she'd never experienced much of anything in terms of ailments. Not even a stay in a hospital, except to give birth to Samantha. With her eyes shut, she tried not to think about the uncomfortable feeling she was experiencing, or the possible reasons why it was happening.

When the truck stopped, she heard voices. Next, she heard people asking her questions and hands grabbing her arms and shoulders to help guide her out of the truck. Bess finally opened her eyes to see herself being lowered into a wheelchair by two male nurses. No sooner had she been placed in the wheelchair than she was whisked into the main building by Nurse Lucy.

Once through the front doors, she went by a few residents, who looked at her with concerned expressions. One even covered her mouth. Bess closed her eyes to avoid the looks of concern and tried to remain calm. She was working hard to control her emotions and the expressions she saw weren't helping. When they finally reached the nurse's office, Bess opened her eyes in time to see Nurse Lucy securing a blood pressure strap on Bess's arm. She pumped it, examined the numbers, then listened to Bess's heart. Without hesitation, she grabbed a large bottle of liquid and handed it to Bess.

"You are drastically dehydrated, Mrs. Bullock," Nurse Lucy explained.

"Is that what's wrong?" Bess asked.

"I'm afraid so," Nurse Lucy nodded. "This summer I've been seeing a lot of this. Now I want you to drink this bottle and when you're done you're going to drink another one. As soon as we get your fluids up you'll start feeling better."

Bess took a mouthful of water from the bottle. She held the bottle up to her face and examined its size while she swallowed. She then turned and looked at the nurse and the expression on her face must have conveyed her thoughts perfectly.

"Keep drinking," Nurse Lucy advised.

"I don't think I can do this," Bess sighed, glancing at the bottle again.

"You need to drink the whole bottle," Nurse Lucy instructed.

"I don't care for the taste of water very much," Bess replied.

"If you don't drink…I'm going to have to give you an IV for fluids," Nurse Lucy warned. "No one likes being stuck with a needle, Mrs. Bullock, so just keep drinking."

For the better part of an hour, Bess remained in the nurse's office, drinking bottle after bottle of spring water and having her blood pressure checked in between bottles. After the second bottle, Chet arrived and encouraged her to drink as much as she could.

With each passing bottle, Bess began to feel a little better. After a solid hour of drinking, she felt like her old self again.

"How are you doing?" Nurse Lucy asked.

"I'm feeling much better," Bess replied. "I can tell I'm going to need to use the bathroom soon. May I go back to my room now?"

"Try to stand up for me," Nurse Lucy said, her eyes fixed on Bess.

Bess nodded and quickly got out of the chair and stood straight up. She even bent her knees and did a little dance before smiling at the nurse. The dizziness was gone.

"I feel good," Bess smiled.

"You look better," Nurse Lucy nodded, before turning to Chet. "As soon as you two reach your room, I want your wife to drink a cup of water every half hour."

"I'll keep on her about that," Chet nodded.

"Give me an hour and I'll be up to check on her," Nurse Lucy stated, turning to Bess. "You need to stop going outside so much, Mrs. Bullock. It's simply too hot for you. Until this heatwave breaks I want you to stay inside and enjoy the air conditioning."

"Nonsense," Bess replied. "If I go out early enough in the morning for my walks, I'll be fine. This was just...a fluke because I was out too late in the morning."

"That's not entirely true," Chet responded. "Yes, you have been going out for walks, but you've also been going out for other things, too. I caught you a few times going out to check on our house and water your gardens. And then there was that gentleman who played pickleball who needed your help. Oh, and then there was that July 4th picnic the other evening. The nurse is right, Bess. You've been spending too much time outside. Promise me you'll stop going out so much."

Bess looked at the nurse and Chet.

"I agree with your husband," Nurse Lucy nodded. "Right now we're in the middle of the hottest summer in twenty years. You have to respect the weather, Bess, or you'll wind up back here again. Now for the rest of the week, I'm recommending that you stay in the main building. After the week is up, you may go for your walks again. I also want you to keep drinking fluids. Hopefully that will help."

Outnumbered and still feeling weak, Bess simply nodded at the requests of her husband and her favorite nurse. Like it or not, she was bound to spend more time inside.

Chapter 23: EARLY MORNING THOUGHTS

It was a difficult rest of the week for Bess. She walked the long hallways of the main building every morning for exercise, but looking at the same walls and doors wasn't as delightful as green grass and blue sky. After two days, she needed some diversions.

She joined in on two morning sessions of bingo, which she hadn't done in a long time. She also sat in on a lecture from a local college professor who was presenting a book review about a Civil War officer named Longstreet. The name "Longstreet" made her think about the long walks she was missing. She even sat in on a book club, which was difficult to stay awake for but she managed to do it. For the rest of the week, Bess undertook every diversion she could think of to fill the hours. By the end of the day, Bess always returned to the Tranquil Tower, her room and the large bay windows that framed the one place she wasn't supposed to go. The view of the grounds simply made it more of a challenge to accept the wishes of Nurse Lucy.

When Friday morning finally arrived in the Tranquil Tower, Bess woke early. It wasn't a noise that woke her. It wasn't her husband's snoring either. It wasn't even a need to use the bathroom. It was a nagging concern. The thought of Anita and her missing diamonds, and Bess's inability to gather more information to solve the case. Once awake, Bess stayed in bed while her mind began to churn over what few observations she had. She also pondered the possibilities of what might have happened to the diamonds.

After a half hour, Bess slid out from under the covers and surrendered to her instincts. She quietly dressed and slipped out of her bedroom while Chet slept.

Glancing out a window in the living room, the eastern horizon was filled with swirls of red and tangerine. She stepped up to the sink, filled a cup with some water and drank it, thinking of Nurse Lucy with each gulp. She then stepped out of her apartment and made her way out to the elevator which surprised her by opening its doors the second she pressed the button.

When she arrived on the main floor, Bess made her way to the exit. She felt like a caged animal about to regain its freedom. Stepping up to the main entrance, she lingered by the exit for a minute, savoring her chance to escape.

"I don't think I should sweat much this early in the morning," Bess observed before grabbing hold of the door and stepping outside.

The morning air greeted her with a steamy embrace. It felt more humid than the dry air conditioned air she had been subjected to for the week. Despite the sticky air, she smiled at her disposition. She was finally outside.

"Here we go," she told herself.

Stepping out to the parking lot, her eyes were drawn to the sky. The sun lingered just above the eastern horizon, burning off some fog that drifted over the farm fields. When the beams of light struck the thicker patches of fog it illuminated the mist with an amber glow. The scene was almost like something out of a painting, she thought.

Heading out through the parking lot, she turned onto Magnolia Lane. She quickly noticed that no one else was walking this early. In fact, not even a car could be found on the road. The longer she walked, the more she felt like she had the entire grounds of the Honey Hills to herself. The only movement she saw came from an occasional squirrel bouncing along the grass.

Eventually she reached Dogwood Lane, where she was surprised to see that the workers had yet to arrive in their trucks. The vacant scene caused her feet to pick up their pace. After so many days of being quarantined to the main building, the sight of her beloved home made her heart race and her legs tingle.

When she reached her house, she lingered at the driveway for a moment, taking in the view for any signs of change. Once she deemed that everything still looked the same from the outside she walked to the backyard, turned on the hose, and began watering her gardens.

"I bet you missed me," she grinned to her plants.

Under a golden sky, she carefully studied what was growing in each plot. She was impressed with how well the tomatoes and cucumbers were holding up. She could also see that the weeds were getting larger and more in need of her attention. After a few minutes of inspecting the vegetables, Bess turned to her second garden where an array of colorful flowers were growing.

A flurry of bright pinks and violets greeted her the moment she stepped beside the plot. The heat of the summer didn't seem to be taking a toll on anything, she surmised. However, upon closer inspection, she did find a few flowers that held a brown tinge around the edges from the endless run of scorching days.

"Nice to see I'm not the only one who's been wilting under the heat," Bess mumbled to herself.

She walked back to her porch and filled a watering can then returned to her gardens to douse a few select flowers and vegetables with some water. When the watering can was empty, she looked up and spotted a bird flying across the sky. She closed her eyes, took a deep breath and smiled at what she could smell.

"All the good things I've missed," she mumbled to herself.

With one deep breath, numerous fragrances filled her head. There were the sweet scents of flowers. The crisp freshness of country air, unspoiled by car exhaust. Even freshly cut grass lingered for her to smell. The wind splashed across her face again and brought out a smile. She opened her eyes and spotted a nearby tree, where the swishing sounds of rustling leaves stirred from the tree branches.

"How I've longed for all of this," she whispered.

Bess opened her eyes, returned to her porch and sat down in her favorite chair. From her vantage point she could see her modestly sized yard, her garden, and one white puffy cloud neatly framed in the clear blue sky. She smiled at the silence. She took in every detail before the muffled sound of hammering began to emanate from a nearby home.

"Enough peace for one day," she told herself, tapping her hand on the chair. "I'd better head back to Chet and get something to drink."

She stood and stepped off the porch, cut through her backyard and met up with a road that wound its way back to the main building.

As she walked, she took in every detail along the way. She liked this particular road because it bordered a farmer's field. Some mornings when she walked, she would take this road to spy on a mother horse and its foal that sometimes were out in the field. This morning she quickly spotted them when she approached the field. She could see the mare with the foal by her side. Both horses, caramel colored with brown manes, were grazing in the field. Their tails casually flicked while they ate.

Bess stepped off the road and walked right up to a white wooden fence that ran around the pasture. She stopped in front of the fence, folded her arms, and watched the horses quietly enjoying the grass.

"At least you two get to eat breakfast when you want," Bess mumbled to the pair. "And *where* you eat is much nicer than a dining room. You two have a fine place for mother and child to spend the morning."

She watched the horses for a few minutes before resuming her walk back to the main building. While she walked, she kept one eye on the horses, the old red barn, and the rich vistas that the Pennsylvania Dutch countryside provided. As she turned a corner, and approached the parking lot to the Tranquil Tower, Bess spotted a familiar sight.

Just down the road, she saw a woman standing next to a field. It appeared to be the same woman Bess had seen numerous times before. Like her previous sightings, this woman was standing in the same spot facing the exact same field. This morning the woman was wearing a yellow dress. Her gray hair still held the same blue tint that Bess noticed from a previous sighting. The bluish hair was full and hung around her shoulders.

Bess was well aware of the gathering heat, and certainly didn't want to feel dizzy again, but her curious nature overtook her brain.

"I think it's about time I get acquainted with you," Bess whispered to herself.

She quietly made her way towards this mysterious resident. As she approached, Bess noticed that the woman appeared to be looking out on a bean field like she was from a few days earlier. The last time Bess saw her it was on a rainy day but the rain didn't seem to deter the woman from standing in the same spot. Bess quickly recalled another day when the temperatures were close to one hundred degrees. Once again, the poor weather conditions did not deter the woman. She ignored the heat that day and stood in the exact same spot by the bean field.

When she got close, Bess noticed how the woman stood with her hands folded in front of her waist and her mouth hanging open. Bess managed to get within a few feet of the woman before stopping.

"Good morning," Bess quietly stated.

She smiled and tried to make eye contact, but the woman did not reciprocate the gesture. In fact, Bess thought, the woman didn't even blink. She appeared to be in some kind of trance. Her face held no expression. Her eyes remained locked on the field and she simply stood with her arms folded. In fact, she wasn't moving a muscle. Given the fact that Bess had seen this woman in the same state before, she couldn't help but wonder what was so captivating about this location.

"Good morning," Bess said again, stepping beside the woman hoping to catch another glimpse of her face. "My name is Bess Bullock. Lovely morning, isn't it?"

"Greta Cooley," the woman softly replied without so much as a glance towards Bess.

"Can I ask you something, Greta?" Bess began.

There was no reply, so she drew in her breath and continued with her query.

"I live in the building back there," Bess began, gesturing over her shoulder. "There have been three different occasions when I've spotted you looking out on this bean field. Not the corn field on the north side of this building. Not even at the horses in the field on the south side of the Honey Hills property. Always here, at the bean field. Now I've seen bean fields before so I'm trying to figure out why you keep coming back to this spot? There's nothing about this field that looks unique to me. That's why I'm curious about what keeps drawing you back here. On rainy days and on extremely hot days, I've seen you stand in this exact spot. Can you tell me what you find so fascinating about this bean field?"

Bess could see Greta's lips part for just a few seconds, then close. Her eyes started to blink, as if processing Bess's request, then her lips slowly opened again.

"It…it isn't the field I'm here for," Greta offered in a delicate voice.

Bess turned and looked out on the lush green growth filling their view.

"Well," Bess began, "I'm afraid I don't see anything else but beans."

"What I'm looking at is beyond the field," Greta explained, and she waved her hand like she was pushing something in front of her chest.

Bess turned and looked around but all she could see was the field. She even looked around for a stray cat or dog that had possibly caught Greta's eye.

"I'm still not sure what you mean," Bess finally confessed. She took one small step closer to the woman. "I don't know what you're talking about, Greta. What do you mean by…*beyond* the field?"

"Over there," Greta said, pointing at something in front of her. "Over there, on the other side of the field. Over where those homes are. Do you see those homes? I come here to look at the white one with blue shutters and the brick chimney? Can you see that home?"

"Yes," Bess nodded and she pointed at it. "You mean the house on the other side of the field? The one between the brick house and the blue one?"

Greta smiled and nodded.

"Well," Bess began, "it looks like a nice home. What's so special about it? Do you know who lives there?"

"No," she quietly stated. "But I did many years ago. You see, that was *my* house."

Bess turned and looked at Greta.

"You mean...you lived there?" she asked, pointing beyond the field. "You lived in *that* house? You actually lived that close to our retirement home? I'm guessing you've probably seen this place for many years."

Greta offered one subtle nod.

"When I moved into that house there wasn't even a Honey Hills Retirement Community," she recalled. "Back then it was just farm field for as far as the eye could see."

"It sounds like a lovely view," Bess chimed in.

"It was," Gretna nodded. "My husband and I bought it shortly after we were married. The day we moved in, he even carried me through the front door. We were the first ones to live in that house and we were so in love."

"I see," Bess nodded. "So you're here not because of the field...but the house?"

"The house and the memories," Greta explained, still allowing her eyes to linger on the structure. "You see, we had two beautiful daughters in that house. The window on the second floor is where one of the girl's bedroom was located. Her name was Margaret. When I was a young mother feeding Margaret or rocking her to sleep, I'd look out her bedroom window at this field. Of course, it was only visible by day. Some nights, when the moon was full and bright, I would stand by the window, holding my baby, and still look out at this quiet calm field."

"A nice memory," Bess smiled.

"Whether it bore beans or corn, this field and I put many a baby to sleep in that house," Greta continued. "I can remember years later when they first broke ground on this retirement community and took part of my field away. It was like...losing a friend. Now, many years later, I find myself standing on the opposite side of what's left of my field...looking back...wishing I could go back to that house, back through that window and into that bedroom to be a young mother again."

Bess sighed when she heard those sentiments. She couldn't help but think about her small home that she and her husband raised Samantha in. A home that Samantha forced Bess to leave to move to the Honey Hills Center.

"Old age does make us more sentimental about our past," Bess sighed. "Like you, when I moved here I left a home that my husband bought when we were young and newly married. A home that we raised our daughter in. But then, my husband died and my daughter moved out. Pretty soon, it was just me living in the house. That's when I agreed to move to the Honey Hills. It was a hard change for me, but I succeeded."

"How?" Greta asked, still looking at her home. "How did you succeed?"

"Because the day I left my home...I refused to leave my heart with it," Bess explained. "When I came to the Honey Hills, I found my heart again. I met some new friends. I found a gentleman and a second chance at love and marriage."

Bess paused and took one measured step closer to Greta.

"You see, my dear," Bess began, "we all like to think about the past at this point in our lives. We all like to look back. However, please don't forget to consider the possibilities of the future. There are still people to meet. Experiences to have. Possibilities to consider that are right around the corner. Not necessarily across the field."

With those comments, Bess stayed with Greta by the field. The sun grew warmer. Sweat dripped down the back of Bess's neck. She waved a few mosquitoes off her arm. She thought briefly about what Nurse Lucy would say, but stayed by Greta's side, asking her more questions and making conversation about the house on the other side of the field. The house that appeared to be at the center of Greta's thoughts. A home that appeared to hold a direct line to her heart.

Chapter 24: CARDS AND CONFUSION

The following day Bess told the sad story of Greta
Cooley to Rose, Alma, and Flo during another meeting
of Bridge Club. All of the ladies agreed it was a sad
situation.

"My father was a carpenter," Alma stated while
sorting the cards in her hand. "Whenever anyone asked
about his job he'd always say he built houses for a
living. He also liked to say that when a family bought
one of his houses and moved in…that's when his house
became a home."

"A lovely sentiment," Bess smiled.

"I agree," Rose nodded. "Of course, I had the luxury
of growing up on a farm. Back then my parents gave
my husband and me the farm. I loved raising my
children in the same house I was born in. Some of my
friends asked me if I ever grew tired of living in one
home my whole life. I would always say that being in
the same house most of my life was…a comfort to me.
Especially when the children moved away. While
coming to this retirement home was a difficult change
for me, I told myself it was the first and last move I'd
ever have to make in my life."

"I think Greta sounds like she's feeling a bit down,"
Alma observed.

"A correct assumption," Bess sighed while looking
at the cards in her hand.

"Yes," Rose chimed in, "standing outside in the rain
isn't for happy people."

"I wish there was something we could do to help," Alma said.

"Short of a time machine what can we do?" Rose asked. "Someone else owns her house. She can't go back there."

"I was thinking of inviting her here...to join us," Bess suggested.

"You mean join...our Bridge Club?" Flo asked, and her eyes narrowed at the suggestion. "We already have four players, Bess. We don't need an extra wheel."

"True," Bess nodded. She could sense the tension in Flo's voice. Bess tried to remain calm while organizing her thoughts to explain herself. "Right now, we do have enough members. However, one of these days I will be going back to Dogwood Lane. Given this oppressive summer heat, I doubt I'll be able to walk back for every meeting. I already dehydrated myself once this summer, ladies. I have no intention of doing it again. In fact, I'd be willing to skip a few meetings on days when it's too hot. Perhaps Greta could fill in for me."

"If you can't join us, maybe we should cancel the meeting," Alma suggested. "We can always just meet and play when it's convenient for you, Bess."

"Ladies," Bess began, scanning the faces of her friends, "we call ourselves a Bridge Club. The "club" part would imply that we are open to other members. Yet, we don't advertise our little club or talk to other residents about joining. I say it's time we fulfill that obligation."

"So you won't be playing cards with us anymore?" Flo asked.

"Of course," Bess smiled, "just not as often. When it's too hot, or too cold, or too wet I'll share my spot with Greta. After all, she needs some cheering up and who better to do that than you three special ladies. Besides, I also have a new grandchild who will be visiting me soon. I fully look forward to spending some days just sitting on my couch holding a baby instead of cards."

She could sense by the expressions on her friends' faces that she had said the right things. She could feel a smile work across her face after this comment.

"As long as we have four players here," Flo grunted.

"Do you think you'll be moving back soon?" Alma asked

"When do you think your house will be finished?" Rose asked.

"My neighbor Anita told me we could be moving back in another week," Bess grinned. "I'm so looking forward to seeing what they've changed in my house...and what's still the same. While I've enjoyed the Tranquil Tower...it will be nice to be home."

"Anita...isn't she the neighbor who gave you that case?" Alma asked.

"What case?" Bess asked, caught off guard by the question.

"The one about the missing diamonds," Alma stated.

"Oh," Bess quietly responded, "you're right. Anita was the one with that diamond problem."

"And did you ever solve that mystery for her?" Rose asked.

Bess looked around the table at the faces of her friends.

"Not yet," Bess sighed and she tapped her cards on the table. "It's a delicate matter, ladies. The detail that concerns me is the hiding place for those diamonds. It really was a place that I suspect only a family member would know about. Therefore, a family member is my prime suspect."

"And how many family members would that be?" Alma asked.

"There's her current husband, who seems to play poker all the time," Bess explained. "Then there's her son...who has been unemployed for a while. I know Anita suspects the workers but...I'm afraid she's going to find that it was someone close to her heart."

"And who do you think is responsible?" Alma asked.

Bess cleared her throat, sat up a little straighter, and pointed to the dealer.

"Let's play some bridge," she smiled.

Not another word was spoken on the matter. The cards were dealt, rounds were won, and smiles were exchanged. While it appeared that everyone was having a good time, Bess pondered Anita's case in her head. She had a suspicion as to what happened to her diamonds. A suspicion that she knew Anita would not like to hear. However, years of experience told Bess that sometimes a resolution to a mystery could come with a little pain.

Chapter 25: THE INVITATION

The passing reference to Anita's diamonds lingered with Bess for the rest of the week. Every morning she'd get up early and take a walk to Dogwood Lane before the heat of the day settled in. Once in her neighborhood, she'd linger outside of homes and speak with workers to try to get to know them. From her talks, there was nothing suspicious about their character. In fact, the more she spoke with them, the more she realized that the Harden family was a tight knit group. They got along very well with each other and knew their roles for running their construction business. Aside from being good at their craft, Bess concluded, they were just nice people.

With no strong suspects in sight, Bess began to avoid Anita. She made a point of not sitting near Anita and her husband for meals. She didn't care to be reminded of her troubles with this case for fear of losing her appetite. She also began to avoid eye contact with Anita during meals and in the hallways. Then one day, out of the blue, Bess received a phone call with a surprising message.

"Good news, Bess!" Anita's voice announced over the phone. "We're finally moving back. Our house is done."

Rarely does a phone call yield such a strong physical reaction. Yet, when Bess heard Anita's news, it was like the words slipped right down her ear and actually tickled her heart. She smiled at Anita's words and had nothing to say in reply. What was there to say? The renovations to Anita's house were complete. Judging by the tone in her voice, Bess could tell Anita was thrilled about this latest development and the anticipation of returning to Dogwood Lane. The news also made Bess curious about her own house and whether she would soon be joining Anita in returning to their neighborhood.

"Cliff and I are going to walk over to the house this evening to see what it looks like," Anita said. "I was wondering if you'd like to join us, Bess?"

"I would love to see it," she quickly replied. "Even if my house isn't finished, I'd be curious to see what changes they made to yours. I'm thinking that they're going to do the same things to every home.... just to keep them uniform. Once I get a peek at your home I'll have an idea of what to expect in mine."

"Excellent," Anita replied. "Let's plan on meeting at the main entrance after dinner and we can walk over together."

Once dessert was complete, and the last bite of her apple pie was gone, Bess met up with Anita and her husband, Cliff, in the Dining Hall. Despite the news about their home, Cliff told Anita he had a poker game to get to. Anita simply kissed him on the cheek and wished him good luck. The expression on her face told Bess her enthusiasm had not been dampened by her husband's gambling engagement.

Soon Bess and Anita found themselves walking along Magnolia Way under a magenta sky. The evening sun was low, and the air wasn't so hot. As Bess and Anita walked, they began to share their thoughts about the dinner they had and the chef responsible for the bland food. Soon Anita steered their talk to her renovated home and her hopes for what they would find. Bess could tell she was eagerly anticipating seeing the changes. Anita was an optimist, hoping to find good things. Bess's heart was more skeptical of what changes they would find. She wished for an ounce of Anita's optimism.

Soon they turned onto Dogwood Lane, where Anita's house was clearly visible. As they walked up the street Bess was surprised to see a car parked in Anita's driveway.

"It looks like you have company," Bess pointed out. "Do you suppose it's a worker staying late to finish up? Perhaps we shouldn't go inside until they leave."

"I know that car," Anita grinned, picking up her pace. Bess followed her up the driveway. She saw the car door swing open and a young man stepped out of the car wearing blue jeans and a dark sports shirt that matched his short black hair. Then a little girl stepped out, wearing a dress and a bundle of curls. Bess quickly recognized their faces. It was Anita's out-of-work son and her granddaughter.

"So glad you could come," Anita grinned while her granddaughter hugged her tightly around the waist.

"Wouldn't miss it, mom," the young man said turning towards the house. "We were excited to get your phone call. You and Dad will finally get your house back. I can't wait to see what it looks like inside."

"So this is your son?" Bess asked.

"Yes," Anita nodded, gesturing to the young man.

"My name is Tom Mackley," he smiled and he put out his hand for Bess to shake.

"Nice to meet you, I'm Bess Bullock," she replied, surprised by his tight grip on her small hand.

"Good to meet you, Mrs. Bullock," Tom smiled. "I've seen you and your husband out on your front porch sometimes when I visit my parents."

"Which hasn't been all that often," Anita grumbled.

"And who is this?" Bess asked, pointing to the young girl holding Anita's hand.

"This is my sweet little Molly," Anita grinned.

"Nice to meet you, Molly," Bess offered.

Instead of speaking, Molly pulled her hand away from Anita and began to twirl and spin behind her grandmother. Bess laughed at the spontaneous gesture. It was the kind of unpredictable action that young children were prone to do.

"Where's Dad?" Tom asked, keeping one eye on his giggling, spinning daughter.

"He had a poker game to go to," Anita said with a roll of her eyes. "You know your father...nothing interrupts his time with his poker buddies. Not even a new house."

"Not to worry," Tom said, pulling out his phone. "I can take some pictures for him when we go inside. I don't know about you, but I'm real curious. Let's go in and see what they've done, mom."

Anita rubbed her hands together like she was trying to get warm.

"I feel like a child about to open a birthday present." She giggled in a way that indicated to Bess she was not the least bit worried about what they'd find inside.

Anita unlocked the front door before leading everyone inside. The moment the door swung open Bess's eyes were drawn to the floor of the living room. The last time she was in this room with Anita, she remembered there were tarps and paint cans everywhere. This time Bess was pleasantly surprised to see that the mess was replaced with new furniture and a pristine golden rug. Stepping inside, her nose detected a slight scent of paint. Bess couldn't help but admire the fresh coat of baby blue on the walls of the room. The color of the walls caused her heart to flutter. Baby blue was her favorite and she hoped it was going to be the color on the walls of her house, too.

"My gosh!" Anita laughed. "I love this shade of blue. Don't you Tom?"

"Yes," her son replied, pulling out of his phone and snapping a picture of it.

"This color will be much more attractive to look at than the drab white walls that were in here," Anita observed.

"It does look very nice," Bess grinned.

While she followed Anita into the kitchen, Bess kept one eye on Tom and Molly. She spotted Molly running up and down the hallway before ducking into Anita's bedroom. Her father remained in the living room before following Anita and Bess into the kitchen. The three of them lingered by some of the new appliances in the kitchen. Anita led a discussion on the new countertop that met with her approval. Bess was hopeful that *her* kitchen would also receive the same kind of upgrades.

"I hope I don't get charged for all these new things," Anita laughed. "It's like a new house. That's pretty much what this looks like to me…a new house."

"I agree, Anita," Bess nodded.

"Mother," Tom said, walking around the kitchen, "I think this all looks amazing. I walked down the hall when we arrived and checked the bathroom and the bedroom. I think everything looks immaculate."

"I'm glad you like it," Anita giggled. "If things get tough with your job hunting, you and Molly can always move in here with me and dad."

"Really mother," Tom laughed, his eyes flicking at Bess. Judging by the look on his face she could tell he was embarrassment that his mother would make such a comment in front of Bess. "You don't have to make jokes like that in front of your friend. Besides, I have some prospects and things are looking up."

"How long have you been out of work?" Bess asked.

"Five months," he replied.

"And, if I can be a nosey old lady, are you able to make ends meet?" Bess asked.

"Really, Bess?" Anita softly objected.

"I'm just concerned for your son," Bess said with a shrug of her shoulders.

"I have some part time jobs," Tom replied without missing a beat. "I also got a severance package, which helps."

"Daddy," Molly said, walking between him and Bess with a large gold necklace dangling from her neck, "Look at my princess necklace. Do you like it?"

"Yes," Tom said, his eyes dipping down. "You look very pretty."

Bess watched Molly smile before walking back down the hall.

"It must be hard being a single father, looking for work and raising a daughter," Bess said, turning her attention back to Tom.

"How do you know he's single?" Anita asked.

"I saw that picture in your bedroom," Bess recalled. "Only Molly and Tom are in that shot. Plus, this morning I noticed Tom isn't wearing a wedding band."

With that comment, Molly again emerged from the hallway.

"Daddy," Molly said, with a silver necklace around her neck, "look at *this* princess necklace. Do you like this one?"

"Very much," Tom grinned, patting his daughter on the head, "another pretty choice, Molly."

Pleased with her father's comment, she turned and walked back down the hallway.

"I'm sorry," Bess continued, "I don't mean to pry. I just think being a single parent, unemployed, with a child…I can only imagine how hard it is for you."

"We're managing," Tom shrugged.

Anita stepped closer to Bess.

"We try to help Tom out when he needs it," Anita quietly explained. "He doesn't like it but...we help him make ends meet. He says he'll pay us back, right, dear?"

"That's true," Tom said, pointing to Anita. "Mom and dad have been very generous. They were nice enough to buy Molly a winter coat and boots in January. Sometimes they pay for groceries, too. I have everything written down. I'll pay them back."

Out of the corner of her eye, Bess saw Molly quietly emerging from the shadows of the hallway yet again. She quietly stepped between Bess, Tom and Anita then turned like a fashion model showing off three necklaces, all gold. The adults could only offer silent grins in response to the little girl stepping between them. Once she had sufficiently showed off her necklaces, Molly turned back down the hallway.

"That was sweet," Bess sighed.

"Bess," Anita said before grabbing her son by the arm, "I need to talk to my son for a moment...alone."

Bess nodded then stepped back into the living room, admiring the blue walls while listening to Anita and her son talk about the new appliances. She overheard Tom mention a possible job with a local bank that involved technology support for their computers. The son spoke of his future prospects with great enthusiasm, Bess thought. It was the kind of optimistic tone of voice Bess recognized from her youth. The kind of tone she used when she had plenty of years ahead of her and tended to look forward to things. When she approached retirement, Bess discovered that old age forced her to lose that tendency for always looking ahead. Instead, old age taught her to value each day and not just the possibilities of the future.

After a minute, she could hear Tom and Anita's voices grow softer and, Bess guessed, the details of their conversation became more intimate. Bess quietly stepped down the hallway out of respect for their privacy. She paused in the bathroom where she found new carpeting, new mirrors and a new shower. The changes clearly made the bathroom look brand new. Again, Bess hoped her bathroom would receive the same kind of treatment.

Eventually, she found her way into Anita's bedroom. The pink walls were still visible. In fact, Bess thought, there were very few changes she could detect to the bedroom. Standing in the doorway, Bess found Anita's granddaughter, Molly, slipping on another necklace. She studied the child for a moment.

"She certainly loves jewelry," Bess mumbled to herself.

She watched Molly look at herself in the mirror. At first, she was adjusting yet another necklace. Bored with her appearance, the little girl then began to make funny faces and stick her tongue out at her reflection.

Bess stepped closer to her and noticed that Molly was wearing one of Anita's pearl necklaces. The strand of brilliant white pearls hung around Molly's neck and down below her knees. It was her fascination with Anita's jewelry that Bess found interesting.

"Don't you look pretty," Bess observed with her sweetest voice.

"Daddy says I'm *his* princess," Molly quickly stated. Then she looked at Bess and an easy smile quickly left her face. "Are you a stranger? Daddy tells me not to talk to strangers."

"I'm a friend of your grandmother," Bess replied, and she folded her hands in front of her waist. "My name is Mrs. Bullock. I live in the house right across the street. So, Molly, now that we know each other's names…we aren't strangers anymore."

Molly gave a faint smile of approval to Bess's words.

"What grade are you in, Molly?" she asked.

"I don't go to kindergarten until next year," Molly answered, before climbing on Anita's bed and jumping up and down, the long necklace snapping at her face. "I'm five years old. How old are you. Forty?"

Bess couldn't help laugh at the child's guess.

"A little older than that," Bess corrected.

"Fifty?" she asked.

"Close enough," Bess grinned.

"When I get old I want to have *lots* of jewelry like my Nana," Molly explained and she hopped off the bed and walked over to the dresser where Anita's jewelry box was located.

"Yes," Bess nodded. "I can tell you like your Nana's jewelry."

Bess watched as Molly carefully removed the pearl necklace before scooping out two more necklaces from the box and placing them around her neck. She looked at Bess and grinned.

"It makes me look pretty," Molly said.

"You do," Bess nodded. "Jewelry always makes a princess like you look pretty."

Of course, it was the kind of compliment that Bess knew would please a little girl like Molly. She watched her twirl around the room more than once, even though no music was playing. Bess was curious about Molly's obsession with dressing like a princess. There was something curious about this little girl and her frequent jewelry changes.

"You dance like a princess," Bess grinned, sitting down on the corner of the bed. "I believe I'll just have to call you Princess Molly."

Molly stopped dancing and stepped over to where Bess was sitting. She leaned close and her dark eyes settled on Bess. A smile left Molly's face and her demeanor quickly took on a very serious expression.

"Would you like to be a princess?" she asked.

"Of course," Bess sighed, pointing to the necklaces Molly was wearing. "It looks like all of these pretty things belong to you, Princess Molly. I'm afraid there's no jewelry left for me to wear."

Molly took Bess by the hand and her eyes grew wide.

"I have a secret treasure for you, princess," she said with a perfect blend of imagination and innocence.

"A *secret* treasure?" Bess asked.

"Yes," Molly said with a voice as soft as one could use to convey a secret.

"Where is it?" Bess asked.

"I keep it in a secret place," Molly whispered.

"What do you mean…a secret?" Bess asked.

"Don't you know about princesses?" Molly asked, clearly confused by Bess's lack of knowledge on the subject.

"I guess I don't," Bess laughed.

"Every princess has a treasure place," Molly explained, still holding her serious demeanor. "It's a secret place where they hide their treasures. It always has to be buried somewhere secret. That's a rule every princess knows."

"Okay," Bess said, her arms outstretched as she looked around at the carpeting and the furnishings in the room. "Right now we're in your grandmother's bedroom. Where could you bury something in here?"

With that question hanging in the air, Bess watched Molly drop to the floor and begin to crawl under the bed.

"Molly, dear?" Bess asked. "Are we going to play hide-and-seek?"

"I'm getting the treasure!" Molly called out from under the bed.

Bess stepped around to get a better view of Molly's legs sticking out from under the middle portion of the bed. A few seconds later, she saw Molly begin to wiggle her legs and hips out. When she managed to get to her feet, Bess noticed that Molly was holding something small in her hands. She walked over to Bess and showed her.

"These are my secret treasures," Molly stated while holding out her hand to reveal four diamond rings that Anita thought had been stolen. "You can't be a princess unless you have a treasure. Since you want to be a princess...you can have these treasures."

Bess was shocked. She reached out and took the diamond rings from Molly.

"But don't these things belong to another princess...your Nana?" Bess said, holding one of the rings up to her face.

Molly casually returned to the mirror, looking at her reflection and casually slipping on more necklaces.

"Princesses need treasures," she stated in a very matter-of-fact way. "If you don't hide treasures people will take them."

"Molly," Bess said, glancing over to the little girl's reflection in the mirror. "Come to the bed. I have something to tell you."

Molly quickly hopped on the corner of the bed, her dark eyes locked on Bess.

"This is a rule every princess should know," Bess said, clearing her throat. "When little princesses get bigger...and older...and more gray...they need their treasures. They need their treasures to remind themselves that deep down inside they're still princesses. Without our jewelry, us older princesses forget that that we're still…special."

Molly didn't speak. Instead she stared down at the latest necklace she was wearing.

"Now I bet your Nana must miss these treasures very much," Bess said, gesturing to the rings. "While I'm certain you're a good princess, Molly, you mustn't hide your Nana's jewelry. If she's nice enough to share them with you, be a good princess and choose to share them with her. It's a rule that all princesses know, my dear. So now that I've told you…I think you know what you need to do."

Molly looked at Bess for the longest time, then took the rings from Bess's hand. Without hesitation, she turned and walked out to give them to her Nana. When Bess heard Anita's voice burst into laughter and praise, she knew this mystery was closed.

Chapter 26: HOME IN THE FALL

As is the rhythm of life, change eventually came to Dogwood Lane. It came when the residents were welcomed back into their homes. It came when the oppressive heat of summer finally began to wane. It came in more subtle ways when the months began to change. By early October, more comfortable temperatures had settled in. By November, cooler air had finally arrived and Bess found herself using her coat more often. In her backyard, she began to see signs of autumn.

Every day a trickle of marmalade and peach leaves began to drop from the trees and spread across the grass next to her gardens. Under the tree in her front yard, the falling leaves formed a perfectly round puddle of ruby red. The gardens she had nurtured through the heat of July and August were starting to show signs of withering. Despite the cooler temps, Bess continued to take her daily walks. Rather than going for a morning stroll, she found that afternoons were better suited for walking around the grounds. When she'd finish a walk, Bess usually stepped out to her backyard with a mug of coffee to sip. She liked to stand by her gardens, sip from her warm mug, and inspect the last flickers of life in each plot. There were a few things still growing despite the cooler mornings. She often thought that God was particularly kind to gardeners by granting them the blessing of a long goodbye to the things they worked so hard to grow.

Bess had lived in Pennsylvania long enough to know that there were certain months to welcome life into her garden and certain months to say goodbye. On this particular day, as she stood next to her gardens, she couldn't help but think about the comfort her gardens provided for her. In fact, she felt more comfortable working in her gardens than she did working in her house. Though she and Chet had been in their newly renovated home for a few months, she still wasn't comfortable with it. Like her gardens, there were still parts of Bess that were fighting against change.

Walking back in her house, she washed out her coffee mug in the sink before looking around at her newly designed kitchen. There was the granite countertop which, in her opinion, was too showy. The stainless-steel appliances that had too many buttons. The country sink that she found uncomfortable to wash dishes in. Taken as a whole, it was one of many rooms that had changed so much it made Bess feel more like a guest than a resident in her home. Of course, there were instances when it felt like her old home. There were mornings when Chet's coffee still filled the air with a familiar scent. There was the small round kitchen table, still tucked in the same corner of the kitchen, where they still had their meals. Even washing the dishes while looking out the back window to her gardens gave Bess the feeling like she was still in her pre-renovated house.

She walked into her living room where her eyes turned to the canary yellow walls that made her sigh at least once a day. Had the workers taken the time to ask, they would have known that yellow was her least favorite color. Given the size of the walls, it was perhaps the biggest change she had to accept in her home.

Of course, not all the changes were bad ones. The furniture in the living room was new, though the cushions were stiff to sit on. The carpeting was also new, but the golden tint of the rug would not have been her first choice. All in all, the changes made to her home left Bess with conflicted feelings. This was a home changed per the wishes of the Honey Hills Retirement Center. Her changes would have been different.

"How are things looking in your garden this morning?" Chet asked, glancing up from his crossword puzzle book. "Anything still alive?"

"A few things are still green," Bess smiled, sitting down at the kitchen table beside Chet. "I'm surprised at how many plants are still thriving. Of course, the cool mornings have taken a toll on many things. There are parts of my gardens that look brown but some of it still looks like the same garden I planted in the spring."

"Good," Chet nodded before glancing back at his crossword puzzle.

Bess grew silent and her eyes began to slowly look around the kitchen.

"It's not the gardens that concern me," Bess sighed, her eyes locked on a canary yellow wall. "It's this house that I'm still having trouble with, Chet. I swear I feel more at home in my gardens that I do in my own home. Why did they have to make so many changes to our place?"

"I think they did a fine job," Chet smiled from where he sat, finally putting his crossword puzzle down. "I like the changes they made. Fresh paint and furniture never hurt anyone. Besides, coming back to a new house…it's like a new beginning for us."

After this observation, the new doorbell rang. Bess rolled her eyes at the unfamiliar sound the bell made. She strolled by a canary yellow wall in her living room and opened the front door. When she opened it, she could feel her mouth curl up at the corners.

Standing in the doorway she saw her daughter, Samantha, who had a diaper bag slung over one shoulder and a tired smile on her face. In her arms, she held what appeared to be a small baby, wearing a pink cap, wrapped in a soft pink blanket. Bess stepped closer. The child's eyes were closed and she appeared quite content in the bright pink blanket wrapped around her body.

"You're finally here!" Bess grinned.

"I missed you at the hospital," Samantha said, and she stepped closer to the doorway. "I know you and Chet couldn't drive there...but everything went fine. Everyone is okay. I couldn't wait to get here. I had to drop Nicole off at school, which is why I'm running late."

"I bet Nicole likes being a big sister," Bess sighed. "I thought about you so much, Samantha. I prayed you would be okay and now...here you are. Oh, sweetheart, it's so good to have you here instead of talking to you on the phone."

Bess gently placed her hands on Samantha's cheeks and buried herself in her daughter's deep dark eyes. They were the same dark eyes she had trouble saying "no" to as a mother. Now when she looked into Samantha's eyes Bess recognized the tired look of a new mother. While Bess was not happy with the circumstances surrounding the pregnancy, the sight of a soft pink blanket wrapped around a baby made her feelings of disapproval melt away.

"Oh my," Bess sighed and she placed her hand over her heart. "Look at that sweet little bundle on your shoulder."

"This is your granddaughter," Samantha said, stepping into the house. "Her name is Faith…and she's the sweetest baby ever."

Bess stepped back and waved Samantha into the house. She closed the front door and followed Samantha to the center of the room, still smiling at the newest member of the family. She stepped closer to Samantha and gently rubbed the back of her finger on the baby's cheek.

"Faith Bullock," Bess softly whispered to herself.

Samantha walked across the living room and sat on the sofa.

"Come here, mother," she said, gesturing to the sofa. "Sit down and hold your granddaughter."

"What if I wake her? Maybe I shouldn't," Bess said.

"She's a good sleeper," Samantha said with a smile. "I don't think you'll wake her. C'mon, mother, you know you want to."

Bess settled into her new cream-colored couch with the firm cushioning. As she sat, she watched Samantha remove the pink cap from Faith's head before lowering the bundle of pink into her arms. Beneath the folds of soft blankets Bess could feel her granddaughter's tiny body all warm and delicate. She smelled the sweet aroma from the blanket and the baby. She cuddled Faith in her arms and got a better look at her features.

Her eyes, while closed, held small delicate eye lashes. Her pink bottom lip stuck out and the top of her head was covered with a fine layer of hair that held an auburn tint. Bess gently rubbed her thumb across Faith's tiny hand and fingers.

"So sweet," Bess whispered.

Suddenly, Faith's eyes opened. A delicate yawn escaped her lips. Her eyes slowly turned and came to focus on Bess's face. Bess smiled and stared right into her new granddaughter's deep blue eyes. In that moment, their eyes lingered on each other, grandmother and granddaughter, neither wanting to look away. Bess felt as though she could stay in those deep blue eyes forever.

"And who is this?' she heard Chet's voice ask from behind.

"This?" Bess asked, keeping her eyes on Faith. "This is *our* granddaughter, Chet. Her name is Faith. She's a few weeks old and even though she can't speak... she just taught me something very important."

"And what is that?" Chet asked, sitting on the sofa.

Bess looked at her granddaughter then turned her eyes to the bright yellow wall beside her.

"I know I've been complaining to you about our house since we moved back," Bess began. "I've been quite critical of the new furniture, the appliances, even the new colors on the walls. But when I looked into my new granddaughter's eyes just now... I realized that a home is more than paint and carpeting. Home is family. I know this will sound silly but looking at Faith...I feel like I'm at home. Does that make sense?"

"Very much," Chet sighed and he reached down and gave Bess a kiss on the cheek.

And so for the first time since moving back to Dogwood Lane, Bess Bullock finally felt like her heart was at home. The newly painted walls, new rug and new furniture no longer filled her with concerns. While she would continue to adjust to the changes, she wouldn't dwell on them as much. In less than a minute, Bess felt quite at home thanks to the watchful eye of the newest member of her family. Bess and Chet sat with Faith, spoke with Samantha, and smiled at what God had blessed them with.

It was from this small child that Bess Bullock finally realized that a home, on this morning, wasn't just a place with walls and windows. It was a feeling. An emotion rooted in love, family and Faith.

THE END

ABOUT THE AUTHOR

 Allen B. Boyer is the author of two cozy mystery series. His books have been sold around the world.

The Bess Bullock Retirement Home mysteries include *Gumshoe Granny Investigates, Clues Over Croissants, Married to Mysteries, Suspicions at Sunset,* and *Whispers in Winter.*

His second series, The Dupree Sisters mysteries, is set in Washington, D.C., and includes *Death at the Presidents Church* and *Blair House Cat Mystery.*

Mr. Boyer lives near Hershey, Pennsylvania, with his wife, Suzanne, and their three children. He likes to take his children and their dog to visit residents at a nearby retirement home.

www.ingramcontent.com/pod-product-compliance
Lightning Source LLC
Chambersburg PA
CBHW020330260626
47156CB00004B/1461